NIGHTMARE
ABBEY

NIGHTMARE SERIES BOOK 1

Written by David Longhorn
Edited by Emma Salam

ISBN: 978-1986083089
Copyright © 2018 by ScareStreet.com

Thank You and Bonus Novel!

I'd like to take a moment to thank you for your ongoing support. You make this all possible! To really show you my appreciation for downloading this book, **I'd love to send you a full-length horror novel in 3 formats (MOBI, EPUB and PDF) absolutely free!**

Download your full-length horror novel, get free short stories, and receive future discounts by visiting www.ScareStreet.com/DavidLonghorn

See you in the shadows,
David Longhorn

ENGLAND
1792

"What is evil?" asked Lord George Blaisdell. "Seriously, you fellows—what is evil, truly?"

The two other men seated at the great dining table exchanged significant glances. They and their host had drunk a sufficient amount of port wine to remove all inhibitions, but not quite enough to hopelessly fuddle the brain. Fortunately, much of the alcohol had been mopped up by the feast the lord had laid out for them.

"Evil is surely the rejection of Christian principles?" suggested Donald Montrose, a young Scottish writer of satirical verses.

The two older men laughed.

I've made a fool of myself, thought Montrose. *Well, it was inevitable. I should not have accepted an invitation from such a man. I wish I was back in London among my fellow hacks. But I need a wealthy patron, and they are not easy to come by.*

"A very Presbyterian answer," rumbled Blaisdell, raising his wine to Montrose in mock salute. "Your chapel-creeping, Bible-thumping Scotch ministers certainly spend a lot of time condemning sin. Especially sins of the flesh, eh? Never stop thinking about flesh, your average holy man."

The lord snapped his fingers and a serving girl came forward to refill his goblet. She was completely naked except for a generous layer of gold paint, as were the other two girls waiting at the table. At first, Donald had thought they were statues standing in alcoves along the walls of the great dining room. He tried to avert his eyes from the girl pouring wine for Blaisdell but could not help glancing at her obvious charms. She smiled at him, and he felt himself blush hotly.

"Simple lust, fornication, or any of your so-called deadly sins," continued the lord, running his free hand along the breasts and thighs of the girl. "None of them are really more than animal desires, impulses shared by all living things. Evil? I think not. Off you go, Sukie!"

Blaisdell gave the girl a playful slap on the rear and she retreated to her alcove. The lord turned to his guests and slapped his palm on the table to win back their attention.

"No, my friends!" he declared. "Evil is not merely a falling short, a failure to observe some code or other. It is an active force in the world, a darkness at least as powerful as that of light."

Donald was puzzled by the question, and disturbed.

"Do you mean to suggest, my lord," he asked, "that the revolution currently underway in France is an upsurge in this force you speak of?"

Blaisdell looked at the young man for a moment, then gave a dismissive snort.

"Peasants banding together to chop the heads off their betters? Pah! Such uprisings are nothing new. But you have a point, Donald. Because if this revolution spreads, brings chaos to the whole of Europe—well, perhaps that will prove me right. Darkness will indeed triumph."

"Stop dancing around the subject, George," said Sir Lionel Kilmain, the older of the two guests. "What do you mean by evil? Devil worship, perhaps, like that damn fool Wilkes and his friends of the Hellfire Club?"

The lord mulled this over, staring into the blazing coal fire for a moment before replying.

"You are right, Kilmain," he said finally. "Now may be the Devil's time. And yes, a few short years ago the Hellfire Club made great play of toasting the Prince of Darkness and such. It was claimed that the infernal dignitary did put in an appearance at one of their gatherings. But there is nothing new in such practices."

Silly talk, thought Donald. *Perhaps designed to get a rise out of me.*

"Surely," he began, battling the alcohol to choose his words with tact, "only the ignorant peasantry believes in a literal Devil these days? Old Nick with horns, cloven hooves, a stink of sulfur?

For a moment, Blaisdell looked as if he might take offense and Donald tensed. He had heard that the notoriously wayward lord sometimes had his serving men pitch annoying houseguests into his ornamental fountain. But then Blaisdell's broad face relaxed into a grin.

"Scoff away, Donald," the lord said. "I, for one, would not be surprised if Old Nick did not put in an appearance this very evening."

Kilmain gave a half smile, pointed a pale, bony finger at his host.

"I suspect you have a surprise in store, my friend. But please, toy with us no longer."

Blaisdell stood up, swaying slightly, and rested his large, flabby hands on the tabletop.

"What if I were to tell you," he said slowly, "that the monks of the old abbey were in thrall to Satan? According to the locals, they made sacrifices. My tenants still whisper darkly about blood rituals. Chickens, lambs. And even, on occasion, an orphan child. All slaughtered in a solemn ritual on a pagan altar. An altar that my workmen discovered lately while draining an old, mill pond."

Nonsense, thought Donald, *the man is merely showing off.* But he felt an undeniable chill despite the roaring coal fire in the hearth.

"Nothing would surprise me about a bunch of Papists," observed Kilmain, who Montrose knew owned extensive lands in Ireland. "Superstition and shenanigans all the way with your Catholics, I've found—an absurd mix of the Christian and pagan. I've lost count of the number of times some old biddy has put the evil eye on me for turning her family out of their hovel. But what of it? The monks of Malpas were driven out in the days of Henry VIII. And good riddance."

"Yes," agreed Blaisdell, "and my ancestors acquired their lands at a very fair price. But the altar they used for their unholy rituals still exists, as I say, although a little worse for wear. It is, in fact, the centerpiece of a little temple I have had built, dedicated to the gods of pleasure and debauchery."

Kilmain frowned.

"A temple? I saw no new buildings in your splendid grounds," he mused. "And no sign of building work in the abbey ruins. So, this temple must be—"

"Underground!" exclaimed Montrose, then felt himself blush again.

"Quite right," said the lord. "Beneath our feet, in fact. Come, my friends, let us descend into the ancient cellars of long-defunct Malpas Abbey! I have been quite busy. See what you think of my—my very personal conception of an unholy temple."

Montrose, unused to wine of any sort, wobbled slightly as he followed his social superiors out of the room. As he left, he caught the eye of the brazen Sukie, who gave a distinctive wink as well as a smile. Montrose had a sudden, vivid image of her slipping into his bed that night. He shook his head, trying to clear his thoughts.

I must not have lustful thoughts, he told himself, and made an effort to recall his toothless grandmother eating porridge.

Blaisdell led his guests through what seemed to Montrose, in his wine-befuddled state, to be a maze of corridors. Eventually they arrived at a doorway decorated with a Grecian lintel. Kilmain remarked on this, asking if the stonework was genuine.

"Marble, taken from the Sibyl's Temple at Cumae," Blaisdell explained, as he unlocked an obviously new set of double doors. "But there's a stone down here that's far older than the most ancient Greek carving, if I'm any judge."

Which you're probably not, thought Donald, tiring of his host's pretensions to scholarship. So far as he knew, Blaisdell had been thrown out of Oxford University in his first semester for beating up one of his lecturers.

They waited for a few moments inside the doorway while Blaisdell lighted torches from a tinder box. With each man bearing a light, they began to descend into the cellars of the medieval abbey.

"Quite the Gothic atmosphere, Blaisdell," remarked Kilmain. "Very much in fashion."

"Fashion?" snorted the lord. "Perhaps. But I like to think it reflects my own unique taste, uninfluenced by the pulling milksops they call artists these days."

The temple was an opulent display of wealth, a circular chamber fringed with marble columns that—Blaisdell explained—had been imported from Sicily at great cost. The walls were decorated with friezes showing various scenes from mythology. Montrose noted that all of them depicted depravity and violence, invariably sexual in nature.

"Not bad, eh?" shouted Blaisdell. "Your classical mythology is full to the brim with amusing filth."

"I fear our young friend is not so keen on the classics," Kilmain observed dryly.

Donald followed Kilmain's example and placed his torches in a sconce at head height. Meanwhile, Blaisdell walked around the circumference of the room lighting more torches. In a couple of minutes, the room was filled with flickering orange-red light, plus the inevitable smoke. Donald's eyes began to tear up, and he took out a handkerchief to wipe them. As he did so, he thought he saw a small, spindly shadow appear in an alcove where there was no one to cast it. But once his eyes were clear nothing was visible.

"Behold!" roared Blaisdell, making a theatrical gesture. "The altar of evil! Imagine what monstrous deeds those wicked monks performed in this hidden chamber, eh? Let us hope we can live down to their standards, Kilmain."

While the gentry bantered, Donald observed the prize exhibit, which stood in the exact center of the circular space. The supposed Satanic altar was disappointing after all Blaisdell's boasting. Donald had expected something brutally imposing, but it looked like a nondescript lump of limestone or some other pale substance, about four feet high and roughly as wide. The upper surface was flat, certainly, but the rest of it seemed like outworked stone. It was only when he stepped a little nearer that Donald could make out some worn—but still discernible carvings—that looked nothing like the classical Greek and Roman sculpture he was familiar with.

"Celtic," he mused. "Or pre-Celtic—Turanian, perhaps. Certainly, dating from well before the Romans arrived in these parts."

"Good!" said Blaisdell, "Very good. It seems we do have a man of learning, Kilmain. I had wondered. Well observed, lad. But do you have the stomach to put these antique artifacts to its original purpose, eh?"

Donald gave what he hoped was a worldly smile.

"I am sure such pagan relics have no real power, my lord, whatever superstitious villagers may say. The days of the old gods are long past."

Blaisdell and Kilmain exchanged another one of their glances. Donald, suspecting that he was excluded from some joke or prank, tried to look dignified.

"You may be right, Montrose," said Blaisdell. "But let us see."

The lord looked up toward the top of the stairs, and Donald turned to see a stout serving man descending with a bundle in his arms. It was an object about a foot long and swaddled in a white blanket. Suddenly it wriggled and for a horrible moment, Donald thought that it was a baby.

"What is this?" he demanded. "Surely that cannot be—"

Then the bundle emitted a squeal, and he laughed in relief.

"A piglet!" he exclaimed.

"Yes," said Kilmain. "At the very least we'll dine on fresh pork tomorrow. You can't conduct human sacrifices in England nowadays, lad. Too many busybodies around, too much officialdom."

Donald gave a hesitant laugh, unsure if his host was joking. He and Kilmain watched as the servant crossed the room and laid his burden on the altar, then withdrew to a respectful distance. Blaisdell, meanwhile, had donned a black robe like that of an old-time monk and stood over the wriggling animal.

"Surely, my lord," Donald began, "you are not going to actually kill—"

"Silence!" hissed Kilmain, drawing the Scotsman aside. "He may seem playful now, but if thwarted he can turn very nasty. Let him have his fun."

Donald nodded, watching as Blaisdell produced a dagger with an ornate handle from his robe. Raising the weapon over his head, he began to chant in a resonant voice.

"I conjure thee, Lucifer, Lord of Light! Look favorably upon our devotions, O Prince of Powers, and reveal yourself to us!"

Then he stabbed the piglet. There was a final squeal, and bright, arterial blood seeped out of the swaddling and pooled on the altar. Donald, having grown up on a farm, could not help but feel a pang of sympathy for the young animal. And, for the first time, the pure contempt he felt for decadent aristocrats like Blaisdell and Kilmain rose to the surface of his mind.

How typical of the idle rich, he thought. *To take the life of a defenseless beast for fun. I despise these people. I would not accept this man's patronage if he offered it.*

Time passed. The blood that had spread over the altar began to darken. Kilmain gave a quiet chuckle. It seemed apparent that nothing was going to happen, and Donald had to suppress a desire to laugh. Then he gave a yelp and clapped his hands over his ears. The air was torn by a high-pitched sound, somewhere between a shriek and a whistle. A few months earlier, Montrose had witnessed a sudden escape of steam from one of the new engines used to pump water out of mines. The intense, piercing sound now assailing his ears was even worse.

The sound ended as suddenly as it had begun. Donald felt a ringing in his ears, removed his hands from the sides in a gingerly fashion in case the noise resumed. Looking around he saw that Blaisdell was trying to say something to Kilmain, but the Irish landowner shook his head. They were all clearly all deafened. But after half a minute or so, their hearing began to return.

"What the hell was that?" demanded Kilmain, sounding annoyed.

"One of your tricks, Blaisdell?"

"Shush, man!" returned the lord, holding up a finger. "No tricks! Do you hear? What is that?"

A quiet, barely audible sound was becoming perceptible over the crackling of the torches. It was a gentle rustling, like someone trying to walk stealthily over dry leaves. Donald looked around the room but saw no sign of movement. Then he glimpsed a dark form appear for a split second around the side of the altar, on the same side where Blaisdell stood. He got the impression of something that might have been a head.

But there were no eyes, he thought, starting back towards the stone steps. *Can't have a head without eyes.*

"What is it, lad?" asked Blaisdell, glancing at the floor around him, his voice betraying nervousness. "What did you see?"

"There was something, perhaps an animal," Donald replied. "It looked at me around the side of the altar. It must have been around your feet, my lord."

"Nothing here now," Blaisdell said, but he moved quickly away from the altar.

"Ghost of the piglet, perhaps," suggested Kilmain. But despite the sarcastic remark, he sounded unsure of himself.

"That sound," Donald said. "Has it happened before?"

"We never done this before, sir," replied the servant, who had backed halfway up the stairs. "Never should have meddled."

"Oh, shut up man!" bellowed Blaisdell. "You're as bad as the villagers. Clearly, we have failed to conjure the Evil One, but perhaps we heard a soul screaming in purgatory, eh?"

Kilmain's eyes widened at the suggestion.

"It reminds me of the Irish tales of the banshee," he said. "A screeching spirit. Invisible, some of the time."

"And what does this banshee do?" asked Donald, timidly.

"Portends the death of a person of note," Kilmain replied. "The peasants love stories in which the banshee heralds the demise of a cruel landlord. But that is in Ireland, of course. No reason for it to manifest itself here in England."

Again, thought Donald, *your tone is less confident than your choice of words. Perhaps you fear the cruel landlord's fate?*

"Oh, come in," said Blaisdell, starting to climb the cellar stairs. "Enough of these fireside tales for infants and addle-pates. We can finish another bottle or two of port, eh? What do you say, gentlemen?"

"I fear I must retire for the night, my lord," said Donald. "I am not as used to strong drink as you."

"Pah! What about you, Lionel?" demanded the host.

"Lead on, George," replied Kilmain, apparently recovering his good spirits. "I will help you demolish a bottle—or a cask, if you like!"

Donald was the last to leave the cellar, and felt a disturbing sense of being watched as he reached the doorway. It was a chill sensation in the back of his neck, causing the small hairs to rise.

Don't look back, he told himself. *No need, nothing there.*

He glanced back, unable to stop himself, and saw only the circle of guttering, smoking torches and the crudely worked slab of stone in the center. It was as he turned his gaze away from the so-called temple that he glimpsed a movement near the altar. He paused in the doorway, twisting his head around to stare directly. There was nothing there, of course. The altar was bare.

Did the servant remove the piglet's body? He must have.

"Come on, lad, your bed-warmer will be getting cold," roared Blaisdell from up ahead.

Donald hurried through the door, resolved not to ask about the dead piglet.

***

"What do you think of our young friend?" Blaisdell asked.

"He can't take his drink, that's for sure," replied Kilmain. "He looked distinctly green about the gills when he went off to bed."

Blaisdell laughed and held up his glass for a refill. It was well after midnight. The gilded serving girls were stifling yawns and shivering a little. The candles on the dining table had long since burned down, leaving pools of wax smearing the silver candelabra. The only light now came from the great fireplace. But the two gentlemen continued to drink and talk.

"Did you really expect the Devil to appear, George?" Kilmain asked. "It seems most improbable."

Blaisdell shrugged and pulled Sukie down onto his lap after she had poured his wine. Gold theatrical paint smeared over his velvet waistcoat.

Too drunk to notice, thought Kilmain. *Or too rich to care.*

"To tell you the truth, Lionel," said the English lord, running a hand over Sukie's thigh, "I was not quite sure. I was raised by religious tutors. Fear of hellfire, eternal damnation, was beaten into me from my toddling days. One never quite escapes that, no matter how fiercely a man may rebel against his upbringing."

Kilmain raised an eyebrow in genuine surprise.

"Quite an admission, George. You implored Lucifer to materialize so that he wouldn't? So you could convince yourself that he does not exist?"

Blaisdell nodded thoughtfully, staring into the fire. Then he pinched the chin of the girl on his lap.

"What do you say, Sukie? Is there a Devil?"

Sukie gave a slightly nervous laugh, clearly unsure how to respond.

"If there is such a one," she said finally, "he is more likely at work in France nowadays, like the Scottish gentleman said."

"A good answer," commented Kilmain, holding up his own glass for his own attendant. "Here, Lizzie, move your arse—I'm dying of thirst."

Kilmain waited for a few moments, but no serving girl appeared. He twisted in his seat and looked round. Lizzie was standing just behind his chair, pitcher of wine in hand, but showed no sign of responding to his order.

Taking the living statue thing too seriously, Kilmain thought. *Silly girl seems to be daydreaming.*

Before he could rebuke her, Lizzie dropped her pitcher, the earthenware vessel shattering on the floor. Wine splashed around Kilmain's shoes, and he leaped up, cursing the girl for her clumsiness. Instead of responding, she started to back away, raising her hands, eyes wide and staring.

"God preserve us!" said Blaisdell in a small voice. He, too, along with Sukie, was now staring past Kilmain towards the entrance of the room. Kilmain turned and saw the Devil. Framed in the doorway was a reddish-brown figure, crouching to allow its curved goat horns to pass under the lintel. It was reddish-brown, cloven-footed, shaggy with clumps of black hair. It was the Devil of a thousand medieval pictures and carvings, the Satan of Dante and Milton. Its face was goat-like, smiling evilly, the eyes slits of orange fire. At the end of hugely muscled arms, its hands sported wicked black talons.

The Devil took a step forward, bringing it closer to the fire, illuminating every warped and obscene detail of its anatomy. The women screamed. Sukie began to mutter to herself, her eyes shut tight. Kilmain caught snatches of the Lord's Prayer. The hideous apparition took another step forward, evidently unhindered by holy phrases.

Impossible, Kilmain thought, anger rising. *A stupid joke. It must be.*

"Did you hire this fellow from the same theater where you got these girls?" he demanded, turning on his host. "You insult me, George. This is crude beyond—"

Kilmain paused, seeing his host's pale face. Blaisdell looked utterly terrified. A pool of dark fluid was spreading over the fabric of the chair between the lord's hefty thighs.

If he's feigning fear, he's the finest actor in England.

"You summoned me. I have come to take you to Hell!"

The voice was bestial, mocking. Kilmain hesitated, looked again at the monstrous figure that was now just a few strides away, reaching for him. He glanced at a plain wooden box on the mantel above the fireplace, knowing it contained Blaisdell's dueling pistols. He grabbed Lizzie, shoved her towards the nightmarish intruder, then made a dash for the guns.

***

Donald had forgotten to wind his watch, so when he arose to answer a call of nature, he could only be sure that it was well after three in the morning. He vaguely recalled climbing the grand stairway to his room, very much the worse for drink. The effects of the port wine were still apparent. He untangled himself from the heavy cotton sheets and flinched slightly as his feet touched the cold, wooden floor. The fire in his bedroom had died down, so that the room was barely visible in the faint glow of coals. He could hear muffled noises from downstairs—shouts, raucous laughter.

Drunken revelry.

Donald used the commode and then, rather than go straight back to bed, went to the window. It was a cloudy, rain-swept April night. He could make out nothing but a wedge of light cast from the dining room window onto the lawn. It was clear that his host and probably Kilmain were still carousing. As Donald watched he saw a shadow appear, evidently cast by someone moving close by the great French windows.

Now, whose shadow is that? They must be very drunk, whoever they are, prancing around like that. Or perhaps Blaisdell is forcing one of his girls to perform? Kilmain said they were actresses or dancers.

The person casting the shadow seemed to crouch, then leaped with remarkable agility. At the same moment, there was a crash of breaking crockery and an outburst of shouting. More shouting, followed by a scream, presumably that of a woman but Donald was not entirely sure.

Decadence and debauchery, Donald thought. *All the rumors are true. Blaisdell is just another silly lord squandering his inheritance on drinking, whoring, and a little amateurish Satanism.*

Another shadow appeared, this one evidently cast by a man walking backwards, arms raised up in front of him. A smaller figure leaped onto the man's back. There was a yell, another crash, more yells and screams. Donald became concerned.

Perhaps things are getting out of hand. But what can I do? Other than take notes for another satire on the idle rich?

He made for the bedroom door but then stopped, gripped by indecision. He imagined himself walking in on a full-blown orgy, clad in his cheap nightshirt, every inch the impoverished scribbler come to gawp at his social betters. As he hesitated, the alarming cacophony from below died away. Donald went to the door and opened it a half-inch, straining to hear. His bedroom opened onto a balcony that in turn looked out over the central atrium of the great house, with the entry to the dining room one floor below. There was no sound. It was pitch black, not a single candle to cast light on the scene.

"Oh, to hell with the lot of them," he muttered to himself. Then he started back. The door was being pushed open. In the waning glow of the fire, he could just make out a small, lithe form as it came noiselessly into the room. His unexpected visitor was naked, undeniably feminine in form, but a thick fall of dark hair almost concealed the face. He could just make out a snub nose and a broad, full-lipped mouth.

"Sukie?" he asked.

By way of reply, the interloper raised a slender hand and placed her fingers on his lips. Her other hand ran over his chest, down toward his loins. Donald made a feeble effort to retreat, but she pressed herself even closer. Confusion reigned in the young man's mind, not helped by a collision with a bedside table. A pitcher of water fell onto the floor and Donald slipped, landed heavily on the bed. The intruder sprang on top of him. The great mass of hair dangled in his face.

"This is—this is most improper," he said feebly.

In reply, the visitor gave an odd, dry cackle.

"Most improper. But it's what you want!"

The voice was rasping, as if the throat repeating his words was devoid of moisture. Donald wondered if Sukie had some kind of ailment. She certainly did not sound like a healthy young woman.

She might have the French pox, he thought. *What if I caught syphilis? You go blind and insane!*

Donald had a sudden, terrifying vision of lunatics on display at Bedlam in London, many of them covered in syphilitic sores. No early morning tumble, even with Sukie, was worth that degree of risk. He tried to shove the girl away, but she simply clung to him all the tighter and began to lift his nightshirt. Her strength startled him, scared him a little. Bizarrely he felt the seductress had become an assailant.

"Get off me, Sukie!" Donald shouted. "I'll have none of you!"

For a moment, it seemed as if his words had succeeded where physical force had failed. The figure above him became unnaturally still. Then the unpleasant cackling laugh came again.

"But I'll have some of you!" said the rasping voice.

Panic seized Donald and, with a huge effort, he managed to free himself. As Sukie lunged at him, he grabbed her by the hair, planning to hold her at bay. But great swathes of hair simply came off in his hand, along with what looked like a layer of scalp.

"Oh my God!" Donald yelled, trying to retreat, only to fall onto the floor, winding himself.

With much of her hair gone, the being that leaped onto him could be seen for what it was—a close facsimile of a young woman, one that could pass for human in the dark. The face that pushed into Donald's had the look of a waxen mask, with a rudimentary lump of nose, gaping holes where its eyes should have been. Its mouth was no longer that of a voluptuous young woman but a round, funnel-like protuberance. The sober, rational part of Donald's mind wondered how such a thing could speak at all.

"What are you?" he screamed, struggling vainly in the monster's grip. He struggled to recall passages from a Scripture concerned with banishing evil spirits. "Are you a demon? I abjure you depart in the name of our Lord Jesus Christ! Begone, foul thing!"

The weird mouth parts extended, tentacle-like, roaming over his face before settling over his left eye socket. There was a vile sucking noise, and Donald screamed out in pain as blood gushed over his cheek. Then it tore out his other eye. The pain was so excruciating that he felt sure he would pass out, but somehow the agony continued.

Donald was aware of his inhuman attacker releasing its grip and put his hands to his face. His fingertips found the empty sockets. He cried out not just in pain but also at the insanity of it all. He howled until he found himself gasping for breath and sobbing, half-choked on his own blood.

"Yes! It is what you most feared!"

Donald froze at the words, his terror almost driving the pain from his mind. He felt his grip on sanity start to fray.

It's still here! Oh Jesus, it's going to kill me now. Let it be quick at least, let it be quick.

But instead of finishing him off, it whispered a few words in his ear. What was left of Donald's rational mind, just before it was submerged in a dark ocean of mental chaos, recognized the phrase as a kind of self-fulfilling prophecy.

"You will be blind and mad in Bedlam!"

CHAPTER 1:

A PARANORMAL PARTNERSHIP

"Naturally, the foundation will cover all your expenses," said Ted Gould, as a discreet waiter seated them at a corner table. "We're very keen on this partnership."

Matt McKay looked around the restaurant. It was classier than what he was used to, even before you took into account higher British prices. When he glanced at the menu, he felt relieved that Gould's employers were paying. They made small talk, ordered, then got down to business while waiting for the first course.

"I'm grateful for this opportunity, of course," said Matt, choosing his words carefully. "But I'm still not clear as why the Romola Foundation wants to team up with a show like ours?"

Gould, a plump, bald Englishman in his mid-fifties, raised an eyebrow.

"Don't we both investigate the same phenomena, albeit in different ways?"

And on very different budgets, Matt thought, glancing at the prices again.

"True," he said, "but 'America's Weirdest Places' is an entertainment show. Clue's in the title. Sure, we make a professional product, but it's basically about going to haunted houses and getting some footage that gives people a thrill."

"Quite," returned Gould, taking a sip of mineral water. "But what makes your show different from a dozen others is that you seek out the less obvious, the more bizarre. That derelict funfair in Utah, for instance. Excellent episode. Atmospheric, well-paced—I'm surprised you didn't win some kind of award."

"But nothing really happened," Matt pointed out. "We gave our audience the back-story—in this case, the fatal accident on the roller coaster—and then our psychics experienced stuff. There were noises at night, shadows, like you said, lots of atmospheric shots. But that's it. Don't get me wrong, I loved the show like my own child, but we're not scientists, we're entertainers."

"Which is precisely why we scientific investigators need you," Gould said. "For a long time, we've been sniffy about show business, and popular conceptions of the paranormal. And a fat lot of good it's done us! Some of us think the time has come to stop being so poo-faced about it and get ourselves a much higher profile. The Romola Foundation was set up in 1865, Matt, and still hasn't found conclusive evidence of psychic phenomena."

But you've certainly spent a ton of money looking, thought Matt. *And I need some of that action.*

"You don't need to persuade me to bring my team over here, Ted," he said. "But why not use a home-grown outfit? Every country has ghost hunting shows, stuff like that? Especially here—isn't England the most haunted country on earth?"

Gould's amiable features froze for a split-second before he smiled again and waved away the suggestion.

"We've looked into it, believe me," he said, "but none of our British production companies were interested in Malpas Abbey. It's not really on anyone's radar as a haunted house, you see. Nobody has stayed there in decades."

Not exactly a lie, Matt thought. *But not strictly true, either. You can't kid a kidder. What are you hiding, Ted?*

The waiter returned with fashionably small portions of food on square plates. During the lull in conversation, Matt noticed Gould absentmindedly rubbing his right wrist. He caught a brief glimpse of a white streak before the older man's shirt cuff fell back into place.

An old scar, and a bad one, Matt thought. *Another little mystery. But here I am in one of the most expensive restaurants in London being offered a ton of cash. Am I going to argue?*

"So, Ted," the American said, picking up an elegant silver fork, "shall we talk dates?"

***

"Seriously?" asked Benson. "People spend their time and money on this—this half-baked nonsense?"

"All good clean fun," responded Gould, picking up the remote to stop the recording. "And these are just the edited highlights. The cases in which we have found—well, enough to arouse our interest."

Benson, chairman of the Romola Foundation's board, grunted noncommittally. He was a spare, silver-haired man of around seventy, well-preserved and sharp-witted. He and Gould were seated in a small theater at the organization's London headquarters. The lights were dimmed, but they did not sit in darkness. Absolute darkness was never permitted anywhere in the building. The walls of the room were decorated with pictures of paranormal phenomena, all photographs or stills from amateur movies. All had been verified as fakes, mute reminders of the importance of skepticism.

"I see shadows, flickers of movement, shapes—some suggestive," he conceded. "But wouldn't we see the same phenomena in any of these absurd shows?"

Gould shook his head.

"Not according to our analysts."

He began to fast forward, stopped, froze a scene. It had been taken with a night-vision filter, the whole screen was black or garish, fluorescent green. A pretty, fair-haired woman was in the foreground, facing to one side, evidently speaking to someone out of earshot. In the background was a circular aperture, perhaps a drain. Gould fiddled with the remote, zooming in clumsily on the opening. Benson leaned forward.

"Hard to judge the height," he murmured. "But that is possibly a child?"

Gould began to move the clip on, one frame at a time. The shadowy figure in the opening seemed to change shape, unfolding to become taller, more spindly. As it emerged, it moved so quickly that it left blur lines. Then it vanished.

"No doubt about that, I think," Gould said flatly. "It's one of them. And it keeps happening. At least three times, with several more possible occurrences. Nothing like this has been seen in any similar series."

"And you really can't say which member of the team is triggering the crossover?" asked Benson. "After all, one could cross-reference the personnel on a given episode—"

"Of course, we thought of that," said Gould, a little testily. "They have had the same core team for two years, made dozens of episodes. It's one of them, but we don't know which."

"That woman," Benson said, referring to a printed sheet. "She's the presenter, Denise Purcell? And there are two others who regularly appear. Both self-proclaimed psychics?"

Gould nodded.

"I think at least one member of that team triggers intrusions without realizing it. They're all focused on more conventional ideas— apparitions, poltergeists. Nothing I've seen suggests they are aware of the Interlopers, let alone how dangerous they can be."

Benson looked from his subordinate to the screen, then back again.

"Very well, Edward," he said. "I will sign off on this one and keep the board off your back. Dangle your bait as you please. Let's hope that nothing too dangerous takes a bite at it."

The informal meeting was adjourned, no records having been kept, as was customary. Officially, Benson was a hands-off chief executive, never intervening in the work of investigators like Gould. In reality, Gould knew that Benson knew everything and watched everyone.

***

"Why are British freeways so bendy?" asked Frankie Dupont. "We keep kind of swooping to the right and left, instead of going straight ahead."

"Probably because they had to avoid so many stately homes, historic sites," suggested Marvin Belsky, leaning forward from the back seat. "Can't just put a road through Stonehenge or Windsor Castle, right Jim?"

Jim Davison, the foundation's driver and general helper, laughed and shook his head.

"Good try, Marvin, but no," he said. "These motorways were deliberately built with curves to stop drivers falling asleep at the wheel. You have to keep moving your hands, just a little, see? Otherwise you'd go straight off into the landscape. They'd spotted the problem with your freeways. And German autobahns, of course."

Marvin looked slightly peeved at being corrected and Denny felt a twinge of satisfaction. Ever since the team had arrived in England, Marvin had been delivering impromptu lectures about what he called 'the old country'. He claimed some kind of aristocratic heritage. Frankie had already annoyed him by asking if he was related to the Yorkshire Belskys.

"Are we there yet?" demanded Brie Brownlee, the younger of the psychics currently appearing on 'America's Weirdest Places', "We've been driving, like, forever. And the cell signal keeps dropping out."

"Shouldn't you know that already, darling?" Jim shot back, with a mischievous grin at Frankie. "Or are your powers intermittent?"

Brie sighed.

"I sense spirits, I don't read minds," she said with heavy emphasis. "If you want all that Vegas stuff, try Mister Belsky."

Sandwiched as she was between Brie and Marvin, Denny felt the latter take in a deep breath. Wanting to avoid another pointless dispute over all things paranormal, she started to fire-off questions about their destination at Jim.

"So how big is this place? Is it very run down? Is the power on, or will we be using lamps? And can we shower when we get there?"

"Whoa, Nellie!" exclaimed Jim. "I've never even been there. I'm relying on GPS to find the way. But from what I hear, the place is a bit decrepit. Nobody lives there, just a caretaker who's based in the village, because—"

"Because nobody dares spend the night," completed Marvin. "We know."

The GPS system told Jim to turn off the motorway, and sure enough a moment later a sign appeared. Arrows pointed to the city of Chester, plus a variety of more obscure place names. Malpas was not among them. When Brie pointed this out Jim explained that the village was simply too small.

"But it's not that remote," he said. "You're about ten miles outside Chester, which is a nice enough place. When you're finished at the Abbey you could do a bit of shopping, see the sights."

"Sounds cool!" said Brie. "I love buying knick-knacks, little gifts for my boys. Maybe they'll have some Harry Potter stuff! Did they make the movies around here?"

"Not that I know of," said Jim. "How old are your boys?"

"Well," Brie replied, "one's just turned six, and the other's forty-three—my husband's the immature one."

As the two chatted, Frankie took out a lightweight camera and started to film the old city. Chester was picturesque, Denny thought. But after the flight plus a two-hour drive from Manchester airport, she was ready for rest, not sightseeing. She hoped Malpas Abbey would not be too Spartan. Matt had not been very specific about facilities.

"Getting closer," muttered Marvin. "I can feel it. Kind of pressure building up. The way some people sense a storm coming."

Aha, thought Denny, *we've reached the ambiguous remark stage. He's limbering up for the performance.*

"I feel fine," chirped Brie. "The sun's shining, and we're on an adventure. I only hope we can help some poor souls move on from the earthly plane."

"You're clearly one of life's optimists," remarked Jim. "They've tried to exorcise the house. Twice. Once in the nineteenth century, again just after the First World War when they wanted to use it as an infirmary for disabled soldiers."

"What happened?" asked Brie, as Frankie swung her camera round to focus on Jim.

"Not sure about the Victorian exorcism," he admitted. "But they say the priest ended up in an asylum. The one in 1919 was worse. Two people died. The police concluded that the third man, who escaped, had killed the other two and then—well, entertained himself by rearranging various parts into a kind of collage. The bloke was deemed unfit to stand trial, though—totally insane."

They drove on in silence for a while.

***

"They'll be pissed," said Matt, looking around the archaic kitchen. "They're used to hotels, or motels at least. Not doing their own cooking."

Gould ran a hand along a work surface, frowned at his fingers.

"Could be a lot worse," he pointed out. "There's electricity, a gas range, showers. The previous owners tried to turn it into a high-toned hotel, but—"

Matt paused in his examination of cans and packets.

"But the evil spirits drove them out?"

Gould shook his head, gave a thin smile.

"Not exactly, but things did keep going wrong. And that's all I can say."

"Sure, I get it," said Matt, resuming his scrutiny of the supplies. "You don't want to taint the experiment by putting ideas in our heads. That's the bit I don't get. People can look stuff up online now, you know?"

"True," the Englishman conceded. "But there are a lot of things that don't make it to Wikipedia. Eyewitness statements, recorded interviews. The Foundation has a lot of material in its archives about this place."

Matt stood up, closing the doors of the cupboard, and leaned against the edge of the sink.

"Okay," he said, "it's not quite Buckingham Palace, but it's still an impressive place. I just wonder if—"

Matt paused, frowning, then pointed up above Gould's head. The Englishman, puzzled, turned to look up into the shadowy corner of the kitchen ceiling.

"What?" asked Gould.

"Those marks on the wall," Matt said. "You can just make them out. Parallel scratches."

"Oh," said Gould. "Just the wear and tear you get in an old building. Settling of the foundation caused cracks to appear in the plaster work. Nothing unusual. Parts of this house are over five hundred years old."

"Right," said Matt.

They left the kitchen to continue their tour. As Gould led him out of the kitchen door, Matt looked back at the parallel lines. They were faded, obviously not fresh.

Probably nothing, he thought as Gould led him along a dimly lit corridor. *But might be worth mentioning to the team. Could look pretty spooky in the right light.*

"This is probably the area you should focus on," said Gould, turning a corner. "It's supposed to be the most troubled part of the house."

Matt stood for a moment, looking from Gould to the wall in front of them.

"Troubled by what?" he asked. "The curse of sloppy workmanship?"

***

The Mercedes SUV was almost too big for the country lanes that led to Malpas. On a couple of occasions Jim had to pull over to let a tractor pass, scraping the side of the vehicle against overgrown hedges. Denny dozed off a couple of times, having been unable to get much sleep on their flight. She tried to focus on the passing scenery, but there was little to see but farmland and the occasional cottage. Finally, they arrived at a set of impressive marble columns that marked the gateway to Malpas Abbey.

"On the home stretch," said Jim encouragingly as he got out to open the huge, cast-iron gates.

"My butt will be DOA," complained Marvin. "I'm paralyzed from the waist down."

"Aw, quit moaning," said Brie. "Think of it as a free vacation."

Denny stared out at the spacious grounds of the Abbey. They showed signs of long-term neglect. There were straggling clumps of trees, an ornamental pond that was covered in slimy green weed, statues clad in dark green moss. Then the house itself came into view. Denny gasped. Everything about Malpas Abbey was distorted, out of proportion, and supremely ugly.

It's the vilest place I've ever seen, she thought. *I can't do this. I can't go in there.*

The house did not so much stand as squat amid a straggling array of shrubs.

"Wow," said Frankie. "That is amazing—like Dracula's castle. Cool."

"You think so?" asked Brie. "I think it looks kind of like Hogwarts. Old, dignified. I can imagine lots of venerable wizards giving lessons on spells and stuff in those upstairs rooms."

"Cold and inconvenient," added Marvin. "But I must admit, it's a very fine building. If I have to stay in a mausoleum, let it be a handsome one."

Can none of them see how evil it is? Denny wondered.

Jim stopped the SUV by the main entrance, and within seconds, the team—minus Denny—was approaching the huge ornate doorway. It was gaping open, and Denny was sure she could hear breathing from inside. Long, slow, deep breaths, like those of a huge animal.

The house is alive, she thought. *It knows we're here.*

She scrambled out of the car and started to run after the others.

"Stop!" she shouted. "Don't go in there!"

Frankie was already across the threshold, glancing back at Denny with a puckish grin as she entered the house. The others were close behind, despite the breathing sounds that were now much louder.

"Can't you hear that?" Denny shouted. "It's alive"

Marvin gave her a disdainful glance as he stepped inside.

"It's not a live show, honey," he said, his voice growing faint as he receded into darkness. "Everything is edited."

Denny tried to run, but she was frozen to the spot. Then a monstrous tongue unrolled from the house's doorway, a living carpet of dark red, glistening meat. The tongue wrapped itself around her, lifted her effortlessly, then began to draw her into the maw of the house. She tried to scream but had no breath in her lungs. The doorway grew closer as she made futile efforts to break free.

"Wake up sleepyhead! We're here!"

Denny jolted upright, realizing that she had been leaning on Brie's shoulder. The SUV had stopped. Frankie was already unloading gear and Marvin was standing with Jim looking up at the front of the house.

"Whoa, sorry," Denny said, rubbing her eyes. "I had this weird dream. The house—well, let's just say it was surreal. It seemed like a monster, like it was alive. And hungry."

"Well, if it is alive, it's having a nap," said Brie cheerfully as she unbuckled and got out, stretching her arms and legs with exaggerated pleasure. Frankie was still filming, of course. *And I look like an idiot,* Denny thought, fixing a smile as she followed Brie into the autumn sunlight.

The real Malpas Abbey was nothing like the grotesque structure of her daydream. It was a large, red brick house with two floors. It reminded her of some of the fine old houses they had passed in Chester, only wrought on a larger scale. The windows were tall and narrow, and a small bell tower stood at one corner. There was little decoration on the outside, and as she looked closer, Denny could see signs of weathering and general neglect. Old mortar had fallen away, chimney pots were missing, and there were small cracks and flaws everywhere.

Maybe it's not an evil place, she thought. *But nobody's loved it for a long time.*

"Okay guys!" she said brightly. "Frankie, we need some reactions from the team. Nothing fancy, just first impressions."

Predictably, Marvin repeated his 'gathering storm' remarks almost word for word. Denny knew it would play well with their audience—the two psychics had been chosen precisely because they were opposites in almost every way. Marvin's snarky pessimism provided the perfect contrast to Brie's positive but humorless, and somewhat preachy, take on the paranormal. Or, as Frankie had once put it, each made the other more bearable.

Denny was surprised, therefore, when Brie's turn came, the normally ebullient woman seemed almost lost for words.

"I guess we'll find out if it deserves its evil reputation," said Brie. "I hope we haven't had a wasted journey, of course, but—well, I guess I'll just wait and see."

Over their years of working together, Denny had worked out a series of hand gestures for the team. From behind Frankie, she signaled Brie to 'jazz it up', but the psychic's only response was a slight shake of the head. Brie gave a brief smile, then looked up at the house with an uncertain expression.

"Yep, just wait and see."

Denny shrugged, and Frankie swung her camera round to point at the front door as it began to open. Matt appeared along with a bald, pleasant-looking man introduced as Ted Gould. The team was used to staged introductions, pretending to meet local experts for the first time for the benefit of the show. Frankie gave Denny a questioning look and received a nod in return.

Keep filming, we'll do it live, re-shoot later if it's clunky.

Gould turned out to be a natural, every inch the English gentleman with a wonderful accent. Denny could imagine him as the lord of Malpas, graciously welcoming his guests. Or she could up to the point when he led them inside and through the house's murky interior, and showed them what he termed 'the dark heart of the house'.

"So, this old doorway was bricked up at some point?" Denny asked.

"It's been sealed more than once," corrected Gould, stooping to point out details. "See? The brickwork down here is centuries old, Georgian or Regency, while up here you see twentieth century work."

"Okay," said Marvin. "So, what's on the other side? What did people wall up? Torture chamber?"

Gould shook his head.

"Close, but in fact it's a staircase down to a cellar. It's commonly believed to be the Satanic temple of Lord George Blaisdell."

"Wooh, that's creepy!" said Denny, looking to Brie for a similar reaction. Again, though, Brie seemed subdued, staring vacantly at the wall.

"Getting anything?" Denny prompted. "Sensing a presence?"

Brie looked startled by the formulaic question and shook her head wordlessly.

Crap, thought Denny, *this is not exactly fizzing.*

"Okay," she said, "is the plan to actually bust through this wall? See what's on the other side?"

Gould nodded gravely.

"I hope so. A good swing with a sledgehammer should bring this old stuff down. Then we'll see if there's anything unusual there. It could just be an empty space."

"Let's hope not!" Denny said brightly, turning to the camera. "Because we didn't fly three thousand miles to look at an old-time broom closet!"

She was about to signal Frankie to stop filming when Matt's voice echoed down the corridor.

"Hey, guys? There's something here. Something on the wall."

Denny saw the flicker of a flashlight, made out Matt's face peering up. The group parted to allow Frankie through, followed by Denny and Gould. When Denny saw what Matt was looking at she felt her heart sink.

Aw come on, she thought. *This is so fake.*

YOU LET HER DIE

At first glance, the writing on the wall looked as if it had been daubed in some kind of dark paint. But as the beams from Matt's torch and Frankie's camera light played on them, it became clear that the words had been gouged out, maybe half an inch deep.

"This wasn't here when we passed by earlier," said Gould. "I would take an oath on that."

Denny gave him a hard stare but could see no sign of embarrassment. She looked up at the wall again, wondering which of the two men had created the message and how they had done it.

Quite effective, she thought. *Though it's a bit pretentious. Still, now it's here we've gotta use it.*

CHAPTER 2

WHO YOU REALLY ARE

"Blaisdell had a reputation for hiring actresses, dancers and the like, and getting them to take part in kinky—well, I guess you'd call it role-play nowadays. Orgies on a classical theme—Antony and Cleopatra, Zeus abducting a nymph, stuff like that."

"Gross," said Denny. "So, he was a bad guy?"

"Not exactly evil," Gould pointed out. "A lot of aristocrats were very depraved in those days but had no paranormal encounters. Blaisdell, however, seemed to have gone too far."

The team was seated in the great dining room on furniture that, as Marvin had observed, had apparently given up on life some years before. However, the elaborately decorated chamber made a good backdrop for the routine Q&A, included in every episode of the series.

"So, what happened to this sleazy person?" asked Marvin.

"Well, that's where the story gets murky," Gould said. "One dark night in November 1792, Blaisdell is thought to have held some kind of black magic ceremony."

"Thought to have?" Denny put in. "You mean nobody really knows?"

Gould, smiling slightly, shook his head.

"The morning after, the entire household was either killed, or vanished. The only survivor was a Scottish journalist called Donald Montrose. But he did not tell a very coherent tale. However, a gamekeeper was out chasing poachers in the grounds on the night in question. He said nothing at the time. But that man did claim—many years later—that the Devil had come to claim Lord George Blaisdell."

"In person?" asked Denny.

"The gamekeeper—who was apparently on his deathbed—said he actually saw the Devil, horns and all, through the windows of the Abbey. It was dismissed as local gossip, of course. Illiterate commoners were not given much credence in those days."

"But we are talking about the literal Devil, with horns, a tail, all that?" Denny persisted.

Gould paused, then spoke more seriously than before.

"Perhaps everyone encounters the Devil they deserve," he suggested. "In olden times, most people really did believe in Hell, Satan, as literal concepts, not metaphors. Even cynics like Blaisdell, who mocked religion, could not have been free of the idea of damnation, eternal punishment."

"So, we won't encounter Lucifer ourselves, unless we believe in him?" asked Marvin.

"Personal demons," said Brie, suddenly. It was her first contribution to the discussion.

Non-sequitur, thought Denny. *Let's get back on track.*

"Was Blaisdell the first person to summon up dark forces, Ted?"

"By no means," replied Gould, clearly relishing the opportunity to lecture some more. "From ancient times, Malpas was known as a troubled place. The Abbey was supposedly built on the site of a pagan temple—some standing stones were apparently torn down by the monks. However, it's still rumored locally that a kind of altar was kept in a secret room by the monks."

"Devil worshipping monks!" exclaimed Denny. "I saw that movie!"

"Possibly," Gould said, laughing. "Opinions vary as to what the altar was for, though. Some did indeed say it was for raising demons, devils, evil forces. But one writer claimed the monks used the hidden chamber as a 'place of trial by ordeal'. A monk accused of impurity was locked in there, and if he survived, he was deemed good. But a black-hearted individual would invariably be driven mad, or killed, or whisked away."

"And ever since then, Malpas Abbey has been a troubled place?"

Denny put in.

Gould nodded.

"The house has been occupied without incident—or reported incident—for decades at a time. But inevitably, sooner or later, something happens. Some disturbance occurs, and the residents move out. Sometimes it's just glimpses of what may be generally classed as ghosts. Sometimes—well, it's a lot more drastic than that."

After half an hour, Matt decided that they had enough material, and they moved on to filming the team settling into their rooms.

"We all need to get our heads down, people, get some sleep," said Denny as they trooped up the grand staircase. "Because we're going to stay up tonight, looking for—well, whatever haunts this place."

She had hoped for an enthusiastic response, maybe even a whoop from Brie. Instead, Brie said nothing and Marvin muttered something about 'getting it over with'.

"The team seems kind of subdued," Denny told the camera, moving close to Frankie's microphone so she could speak quietly. "Maybe that message—whoever or whatever wrote it—knocked them off-kilter. But let's hope they're back to their usual selves by sundown!"

***

Brie sat on the huge, four-poster bed and stared at the pattern on the worn carpet.

Gotta keep busy, she told herself. *Don't think about it.*

She stood up, walked mechanically into the antiquated bathroom, turned on the hot tap in the sink. There was a rumbling from somewhere below, and a gout of brownish water shot out, swirled down the plughole. Brie waited for the water to clear, which it did eventually, then washed her face. She did not feel like tackling the shower.

Brie dried her face, looked at her reflection in the speckled mirror. She saw a reasonably attractive woman, maybe a little heavy-set, jowly, but with a kind face.

A good person, she thought. *Caring. Wife and mother. Churchgoer. Supporter of worthy causes.*

"I didn't let her die," she said. "I was young, I didn't know. I never told her to—"

A shadow flickered behind her, cutting off the light from the bedroom. Brie spun around, heart racing, wondering if the intruder might be Frankie.

She wouldn't sneak around, she told herself. *She doesn't like me much, but she wouldn't act like that.*

Brie emerged tentatively from the bathroom, looked behind the door, then checked under the bed. There was nobody else in the room. Her alarm subsided, then she jumped as a fast-moving shadow shot across the floor. It was a bird flying past the window. Brie laughed in relief, went to look out at the grounds of Malpas Abbey. Black shapes hopped on the ill-kempt lawn. She could just make out the cawing of crows.

Or maybe ravens. Aren't they birds of ill-omen?

Brie shook her head, trying to dislodge the dark thoughts that had surged up when she had seen the writing gouged into the wall. She drew the curtains not quite closed, letting some of the September light spill into the dark-paneled room. Then she walked back to the bed, said a short prayer, took off her shoes, and curled up on top of the covers.

Sleep, she told herself. *Got a job to do. People relying on me. The Lord will not forsake me if I am sincere and humble.*

The plumbing began to rumble again, louder this time, and did not let up. She guessed someone had decided to try their shower. She got up and opened a secret pocket in her flight bag. She took two powerful tranquilizers from a small packet, replaced the rest of her stash, and sealed the pouch. Then she climbed onto the bed and drew the four-posters curtains around her. It was oddly comforting.

Like being out camping with the boys, she told herself. *Good memories. Positive thinking.*

When she lay down again the familiar effects of the prescription meds kicked in. The rumbling gradually dwindled as sleep claimed Brie.

***

"You big jerk!" Denny snapped. "How did you do it? Did you cover it up, with a sheet of paper or something? Then pull it off just before we arrived?"

"What are you talking about? And for Christ's sake, not so loud!"

Matt was defensive but angry, holding up his hands in front her. Denny had slapped him a couple times before, during their brief relationship. They were supposedly over the breakup, but every now and again, the bitterness would surge up. Now they were in his bedroom having a fight. It was too familiar, something Denny had experienced far too often.

"That dumb message!" she hissed, jabbing a finger into his chest. "I'm supposed to believe it just appeared?"

Matt held up his hands in a helpless gesture.

"You think I'd be that dumb?" he asked. "With so much riding on this?"

"I *know* you can be that dumb!" she almost shouted. "What about Akron, that creepy doll we so conveniently found in a tire factory that was pretty much the most boring place on earth?"

"Oh, come on, I just moved it into plain sight!" he protested. "I never faked anything, just did some stage dressing."

"That wall was not stage dressing, it was just fraud!" she said, struggling to control her anger.

"I didn't do it! Jesus!" Matt shouted. He was pacing up and down, now, and Denny recognized his martyred air.

"Okay," she said, trying to stifle her doubts. "If you didn't, who did? Gould?"

"I don't see how he could have done it," Matt said, and stopped pacing. "I was with him the whole time since he drove us here. And that wall was blank when he showed me the blocked doorway."

They looked at one another.

"So, it's a genuine mystery?" she asked. "There's nobody else here who could have done it?"

Matt shook his head.

"Some caretaker comes in every morning, but he wasn't here when we arrived. I suppose—"

"What?" she asked, as he Matt paused for thought.

"Somebody could be hiding," he pointed out. "It's a big house, none of us knows it, whereas Gould might have set something up."

Denny turned that idea over in her mind.

"Let's see if anything else happens," she decided. "I'm sorry I unloaded on you like that. Maybe I'm more tired than I thought."

"Yeah," he said. "Let's get some shuteye."

He padded the bed. Denny smiled wearily.

"Yeah, we both sleep a lot better alone," she said, adding from the doorway.

***

"You let me die."

Brie sat upright, confused by the unfamiliar surroundings, disturbed by the dream that was already fading. It took her a few seconds to recall where she was. When she did remember, she sighed. She checked her watch and found she had only slept for two hours. The sun was lower, though, and its autumn light was streaming through a gap in the curtains. She got up to draw them fully closed.

"You let me die."

This time she could not dismiss the words as part of some half-remembered nightmare. The voice, though low pitched and whispering, was disturbingly familiar. It was a girl's voice, that of a teenager on the brink of maturity. Brie felt sure that it was the voice of her own conscience.

She never did grow up. Never got the chance.

Unwelcome memories swarmed in her head. Facts Brie had not considered for years suddenly demanded her attention. Guilt began to take possession of her, a corrosive and all-embracing guilt that she could do nothing to assuage.

"I was too young," she said as she drew the curtains closed. "I didn't know what I was doing."

Brie remembered her awkward sixteen-year-old self, raised in a tight rural community, dominated by the pastor of her church. Brother Charles had declared Brie to be especially blessed, someone who could commune with angels, a child gifted with prophecy. From her childish talk of auras and spirits, he had woven a small-town cult, with Brie as the figurehead. And then things had gotten too serious, too soon, and her parents had taken her away, burned that bridge behind them.

"I know who you really are."

The simple statement sounded like a threat of the direct kind. And this time Brie could not convince herself that the voice was in her head. The room was still not totally dark, since the old curtains were threadbare and still admitted a wan light. In the colorless radiance, Brie saw the faded drapes around the four-poster bed move, just a touch. But still far more than could be explained by a rogue breeze in the old house.

"Who am I?" she asked, surprised by her own courage. "I'm not that naive kid anymore. I've tried to make amends."

"But I'm still a naive kid. I had no choice."

The figure that emerged from the curtained four-poster was almost, but not quite, Marybeth Carson. Of course, it couldn't be. Marybeth had died from a rare kind of leukemia nearly twenty years ago. Died not quite a year after her friend and neighbor Brie had told Marybeth to fear nothing, that God would cure her, that all she had to do was put her trust in Brother Charles. Everyone in their little town knew that the pastor channeled the healing power of the Lord. Everybody in town said so, gave examples, spoke of miracles. But it turned out that Brother Charles had had his limitations, and the doctors had been right all along.

"I believed in him," Brie whimpered. "Everybody did. I just went along with the rest."

The apparition slowly, painfully, disentangled itself from the bed's draperies and stood upright. Even in the poor light Brie could see that Marybeth was naked, painfully thin, and terribly sick. The wasted body was hairless as the girl's skull, and Brie recalled the doses of chemotherapy and radiation that had been too late.

Someone looking that bad could not really stand, she told herself. *This is an apparition sent by the Devil, a trick to make me despair. To make me lose my faith.*

Brie began to recite the Lord's Prayer, rushing through the familiar words as the Marybeth-thing advanced on her. As it grew closer, the revolting creature began to lose much of its semblance of humanity. Great tumors began to erupt from the parchment-like skin, until the entity was a walking cancer, a horrific mass of diseased tissue creeping toward her on spindly, malformed legs.

It reached out for her, and Brie stumbled back until she felt the windowsill in the small of her back. Reaching for her with bony arms, the being's bloated face seemed to smile. Tears streamed from tiny black eyes while the huge mouth drooled.

"I've been lonely, Brie. You were so nice when you visited me, read the Good Book to me, prayed with me. I just want to give you a great big hug."

***

Ted Gould made his way out of the kitchen door and into what had been a Victorian herb garden. He looked around making sure nobody was overlooking him from one of the house's back windows. All of the guests had been carefully allocated rooms at the front, south facing. When he was satisfied, he took out his phone and called Benson to report on the new development.

"Is there any chance the Americans are faking a phenomenon?" Benson asked at once.

"I don't see how," Gould replied patiently. "I was watching the producer the whole time. None of the others had the opportunity, let alone the time. So, it seems that there has already been a response."

"In broad daylight?" Benson still sounded skeptical.

"There are a few examples," Gould pointed out. "If conditions are dark enough. Remember, we don't know if they're strictly nocturnal, or simply taking advantage of the fact that we are visually-oriented beings."

A pause, then Benson asked what he planned to do next.

"Go through with the plan, as outlined," Gould replied. "What else is there? This response supports my hypothesis that at least one of them can trigger a PD event. That means we will at least gather some data, perhaps more."

Another pause, then Benson spoke emphatically.

"Very well, Gould, you are free to use your own judgment. But keep me informed. And if there is any serious risk to the team, I will insist on extraction. Do you understand?"

Gould ran his left hand over the pale scars on his right wrist.

"I understand, sir."

***

The scream cut through the gloomy interior of the house and set Denny racing along the landing. She almost collided with Frankie, who was emerging from her own bedroom, camera at the ready as usual.

"I'm assuming that was Brie," Denny said.

"Could have been Marvin," Frankie shot back, with a wry grin.

A second later, they almost collided with Brie, who was running barefoot towards the staircase. For a moment, Denny wondered if this was part of some conspiracy involving the wall graffiti. But then Brie collapsed against the wall sobbing, and Frankie stopped filming. It took them a while to get Brie to explain what had happened, by which time, Matt, Marvin, and Jim had arrived.

"Something in your room?" asked Denny, not quite sure what Brie was saying.

"I've tried to make amends!" Brie babbled. "I never hurt anyone, just tell them good things, help them feel better about themselves!"

She's in a hell of a state, Denny thought. *God, I hope she doesn't have to bail on us.*

"What did you see?" Matt asked.

"You mean you don't know?" Denny asked him.

"I've no time for your BS!" Matt replied, striding off along the passage. He stopped at Brie's door, looking back at the rest of them, then went inside. Jim got up and started to follow, but Matt emerged from the room after just a few moments.

"Nobody in there," he said. "She must have had a nightmare."

"It was real!" the psychic protested. "I saw her. She was—God, she was dying, still dying after all these years."

"Must have been a bloody realistic nightmare," commented Jim, crouching down by Brie. "Hey, let me help you downstairs? We can have a nice cup of coffee in the kitchen."

Brie stared at him as she blew her nose on a tissue, then nodded.

"I'd like that," she said in a small voice.

"Hey," said Denny, feeling she had not been sufficiently sympathetic, "we can swap rooms if you'd rather not go back in there?"

"Thanks," Brie replied, sniffling.

As Jim and Frankie helped Brie to her feet, Denny caught Matt's eye. He made a motion with his hands.

Pill-popping, Denny thought. *She's still on that prescription garbage. I guess he found her stash. Again. God, this could be a mess.*

Brie might have caught the expression on Denny's face. She looked the young woman in the eye and said simply, "I know what I saw. And it knows what you really are."

Frankie, Jim, and Matt led Brie downstairs while Denny stood watching them go with Marvin. Marvin, who had looked on saying nothing while the drama unfolded, solemnly tapped the side of his head with a forefinger.

"These upbeat religious types—they're often unstable," he remarked, and set off back to his room.

***

"So, Ted, tell us a little about the Romola Foundation."

After the incident, Denny had given up on getting some sleep for now. Jim and Matt were keeping the still-shaken Brie, company in the kitchen. So Denny asked Gould to give some background on the case. Before they began, she explained that the footage might not be used, but would probably furnish a few useful clips. Now they were standing outside Malpas Abbey, in what Frankie pronounced perfect daylight.

"The Foundation was set up by Sir Algernon Romola," explained Gould, "a very wealthy gentleman whose beloved wife died in childbirth. Spiritualism was very much in vogue at the time, and Romola—perhaps understandably—seized upon the notion that he could speak to his wife again."

"And how did that pan out?" Denny asked.

"Sadly, Romola was a very intelligent skeptic, and quickly realized that a lot of spiritualist mediums were simply frauds. Long before Houdini, Romola began exposing common tricks—usually some basic conjuring that was only possible because séances were held in pitch darkness."

"So, he became disillusioned pretty quickly?" Denny put in.

"Yes," said Gould, "but there were just a few instances where Romola, for all his perspicacity, could not find any evidence of fraud. Things moved, presences were felt, and in some cases, actual injuries were inflicted, allegedly by poltergeist activity. Romola was fascinated but also frustrated by these few instances of genuine paranormal events."

"So, he set up a charitable foundation to settle the question?" she asked.

"Indeed," Gould replied, "and over one hundred and fifty years later, we are still grappling with the paranormal."

Not bad, thought Denny, *but a bit ordinary. It needs a personal touch.*

"And how did you become involved with the foundation, Ted? Were you always interested in the paranormal?"

For a moment, Denny thought Gould would give an evasive answer. But then he looked past her, gazing into the distance, and began to talk.

"When I was a boy, seven years old, most Saturdays I used to go out with a group of friends to what we called the forest. Actually, it was a small copse of trees just a few dozen yards across. But it was pretty big to us. It was about a fifteen or twenty-minute walk from the village where we lived. We used to play soldiers, climb trees, turn over stones, and see what crawled out. Anyway, on the weekend in question, some kind of mix-up must have occurred, because when I turned up, there was nobody else there. The forest was deserted. I spent some time mooching around, waiting for the gang to materialize. No dice. So, I decided to go home after eating the packed lunch my mum had made. I sat down on a fallen tree and started unwrapping some sandwiches. Then—and I remember this very clearly—I became aware of the silence. It was autumn, the leaves had started to fall, but there were normally plenty of birds around, plus squirrels, other small animals. But now, there was total silence, not even a breath of wind. The sound of the grease-proof paper was really loud as I opened my little packet of sandwiches. So loud, in fact, that I stopped, worried that I would attract attention. That something would know I was there."

He shrugged, smiling, but Denny noticed that the smile did not reach his eyes.

This could be good, she thought. *It might even be the real deal.*

"Right after the silence hit me like a wave, I was suddenly sure I was being watched," Gould went on. "I could feel the hairs standing up on the back of my neck. And nothing could have made me turn around and look to see who or what was behind me. Then I heard a crackling sound, like someone walking very stealthily through the leaf litter. I put my lunch back in my little satchel and got up, moving slowly."

"Oh my God," breathed Denny.

"Of course, I'd been given all the usual warnings by my parents," Gould went on. "Don't talk to strange men, don't accept candy or get into a car... all that stuff. But I just knew, at a visceral level, that this was different. That if I turned around, it wouldn't just be a stranger's face I'd see. Or at least, not a human stranger."

Gould paused, and Denny—for the first time in years—found herself unable to come up with an instant question. Frankie swung round to capture Denny's hesitation, waiting for the next question.

"So, what happened next?" she managed to ask, after missing a beat.

Gould looked away, then back at Denny.

"I ran. All the pent-up fear just burst out in panic. I ran like a maniac, and by the time I got home, I had a terrible stitch in my side. My mother was there, surprised to see me back so soon. Then she saw my face and realized something was wrong. But I could never really explain it to her. The silence, the watcher, that creeping sound."

"But you didn't actually see any evidence of the paranormal?" asked Denny, feeling the first stirrings of disappointment.

Gould looked away again.

"I didn't, no—I just felt a presence. But the day after my scare, a little girl who lived on the other side of the forest disappeared. She was a little younger than I was. She'd gone out gathering blackberries with friends. They were just on the edge of the forest and they noticed she had gone. Vanished into thin air, that was what the newspapers said. The police found the jar she had been using, but nothing else. Not at first."

"But they found something later?" Denny asked, trying to keep her voice level.

"Weeks later, after search parties had gone over the whole area a dozen times, they found her. What was left of her. She was dead. Desiccated, as if all the moisture had been sucked out of her. The coroner returned an open verdict—that's usual when there's no obvious cause of death. To this day, there's no convincing explanation as to where she went, what happened. What took her."

Again, Frankie swung the camera around to capture Denny's expression.

"Thanks for sharing that with us, Ted," said Denny. "So that's what got you interested in the paranormal?"

Gould shrugged.

"I had almost forgotten it, or perhaps the trauma had induced a kind of amnesia. Then years later, it came back to haunt me. The feeling of being alone in the woods. I was working as a research physicist at Cambridge when I happened to hear about the Romola Foundation. I'd become frustrated with mainstream science, so here I am. And here we are."

Gould turned to look up at the front of Malpas Abbey. Denny knew, without turning to look, that Frankie was now shooting past the Englishman, focusing on the old-fashioned windows, the climbing vines, the worn brickwork.

"I think that's a wrap," she said. "Thanks, Ted. That was great."

"Glad it was okay," said Gould, then turned to walk back inside.

Denny and Frankie discussed the segment, agreeing that it would work with minimal editing. Then they decided to film the house and grounds, including the old abbey ruins. As they moved from one spot to the next, they chatted, and inevitably the future of the show came up.

"So Matt thinks this can revive our ratings?" asked Frankie.

"The big question, the one you never answer—why do you keep doing this crummy job?"

"Because I can't get another one," said Frankie simply. "Newsflash—times are tough for everyone."

"No, no, no!" insisted Denny. "No way. You're a damn good camerawoman, cameraperson, whatever. You make a cheap show look classy. And you know how to edit properly, for God's sake. Why not go for it, get yourself a job with a proper outfit?"

Frankie shook her head.

"Guess I just love working with you guys," she said, taking a sip from her water bottle. "It's the glamor of it all."

CHAPTER 3

NIGHTMARE ON A SUNNY AFTERNOON

After they had finished filming, Denny went back upstairs and switched rooms with Brie. The psychic was now dozing on a sofa in the dining room, covered by Jim's coat, and Denny didn't want to wake her. As she moved Brie's things, she resisted the temptation to search her colleague's luggage for pills, preferring to keep an open mind. But she also resolved to ask Matt if he had found anything when she got the chance.

"Kind of spooky, I guess," she said to herself, standing in the middle of the big guest bedroom. "But not that bad."

Brie, consistently the team's most popular member with their audience, had naturally been given the best room. Denny opened the curtains wide, let what remained of the afternoon light dispel most of the gloom. There was nothing to see but old furnishings, a few faded pictures, and a dark red carpet that had seen better days.

Matt checked the room, she told herself. *He didn't see anyone, so there's nobody here.*

Despite this, she found herself holding her breath as she opened closets and drawers, only to find them empty. The *en suite* bathroom was far too small to furnish a hiding place. But still something bothered her, a nagging doubt. She felt she was missing something obvious about the room, no matter how closely she scrutinized its contents.

I need to rest. Just stop thinking and sleep.

Denny lay down on the bed without drawing the curtains around her. Predictably, despite her tiredness, sleep would not come. Instead, she found herself remembering all the strange beds she had slept in down the years. There had been dozens during the making of each season of the show. Before that, had been the life of an army brat, traveling between bases. Vague memories of her childhood fears began to form, not quite well-defined enough to grasp details.

The dark, she thought. *Everyone's scared of that when they're kids. No biggie.*

Then she sat upright, listening intently. A faint scratching, just barely audible.

Could be rats?

One thing about Matt she had learned. Like a lot of arrogant, men, he could sometimes overlook the obvious.

He looked around the room, sure. But he was awfully quick about it. Did he look under the bed?

Denny began to creep slowly towards the edge of the mattress. But she had only been moving for a couple of seconds when she felt a sudden bump. One of the wooden pillars gave a creak, a furled curtain swayed. She froze. All her childhood terrors were suddenly with her again. Killer clowns, boogeymen, aliens, vampires all merged into a formless, faceless monster lurking in the dark.

None of those are real, she thought. *But there could be some jerk hiding under the bed. Some jerk in a mask, maybe.*

Denny estimated the distance to the door as no more than four yards. It was unlocked. But it was also a big, cumbersome slab of oak, with a clunky knob. Again, Denny suppressed her fears as best she could. She stood up on the mattress, crouching to avoid hiding her head in the four-poster's stiff canopy. Then she took a flying leap, landing just short of the door. She slammed a hand against the door panels, feeling a pain in her wrist as it absorbed her momentum, then grabbed the knob.

Denny had yanked the door open and was already halfway out of the room when she risked a look behind her. There was nothing crawling out from under the bed, no childhood monster reaching out for her, no creep Matt had paid to create some cheap scares. She heaved a sigh of relief, leaned against the door frame. Then she bent down to peer under the four-poster and saw nothing but daylight.

"God, I am such an idiot," she breathed.

Then the frame of the four-poster shook again, and a pale, half-formed face appeared. Its features were incomplete, like a mask of wax in process of melting. It looked down on her from on top of the bed's broad canopy. Killer clown, movie vampire, alien—its features flowed and rippled as it tried out one horrific visage after another, apparently unable to settle on one. A hand waved lazily at her, then the creature withdrew out of sight.

Denny rushed into the corridor, slammed the door behind her, then leaned against it. It took her a few minutes to summon the willpower to run downstairs and call for help. This time she made a point of ushering everyone into the room, hoping that if some trickery had been played Frankie or maybe Jim would spot it.

"Nothing there now," said Gould, standing on a chair to look on top of the canopy. "Here, take a look."

Denny reluctantly accepted the offer. Gould was right, she saw. But then she looked more closely and saw that there was a dent in the canopy that was roughly the size of a small person—a woman or a child. She also noted that the dust had been disturbed.

"So, there might have been something up there," said Frankie, taking Denny's place to film the area. "Cool."

"Not cool," retorted Denny. "Scared the crap out of me!"

She gave Matt an accusing look, still unwilling to absolve him.

"What?" he asked. "You think I'm faking all this? You got crazy ex-girlfriend syndrome, hun."

Gould looked from one to the other, realization dawning on his face.

"You two have a more than professional history, I take it?"

"Got it in one, Sherlock," Frankie called down. "But don't worry, it never leads to social awkwardness."

She jumped gracefully down from the chair.

"So, we done here?"

***

Jim had prepared a basic meal for the team, arguing that pasta might induce sleep more effectively than willpower. When Denny knocked at his door Marvin protested that he had been sleeping perfectly well already, but the offer of food brought him downstairs. Gould, who had eaten earlier, decided to take a walk before sunset. After they had eaten, Jim went to check on the boiler, which was still making ominous sounds.

The team—minus the still-sleeping Brie—was left to review the small amount of footage shot so far. Nothing out of the ordinary happened until they came to Gould's interview.

"He's lying," said Marvin bluntly.

Matt chimed in with an 'Uh-huh'.

"How do you know?" Denny demanded, stopping the recording. "He seemed totally sincere to me."

"Which is how a good liar sounds," retorted Marvin, sarcastically. "Okay, so the guy may not be making it all up, but it's mostly BS. Now, I must go back to my splendid suite. If you want me, I'll be trying to get my shower to work. It looks like it was designed by Edison or one of those guys."

The medium got up and left the room.

"To be fair," said Matt, seeing Denny's annoyance, "I think he's telling the truth as best he can. But he's lying by omission—there's something else."

"Why?" demanded Frankie, showing signs of genuine annoyance. "He could've just said he was always interested in ghosts and stuff. Hell, that's what most people say."

"Why does anyone make up grandiose lies?" Matt said, with a helpless gesture. "But, like I said, this guy has a secret. If Brie was here, she'd say he's got a troubled aura, poor man."

"Okay, maybe Gould is not completely on the level, but what about all the other stuff that's happened?" demanded Denny. "No way was what I saw fake. Or am I a big fat liar, too?"

"No, but you were on that boundary between sleep and wakefulness," Matt pointed out. "In a place where someone said they saw something. Your imagination was working overtime, an exhausted brain."

"Oh, bullshit!"

Denny got up and took the dirty plates over to the sink. Frankie joined her while Matt, wearing a martyred look he had long since perfected, left.

"You wash, I'll dry," offered Frankie. "And he's still a complete asshole, in my humble opinion. Seriously, what did you ever see in him?"

"Looks," admitted Denny. "I'm kind of superficial."

"That way lies heartbreak," sighed Frankie. "It's character that counts."

"Open your eyes, girlfriend," Denny said. "The beautiful ones can get away with anything."

After a few moments, Frankie asked, "So what happened? I mean, what did you see?"

Denny gazed thoughtfully at her friend before answering.

"Would you believe, the boogeyman?"

Frankie raised a quizzical eyebrow, and Denny tried to explain the way so many childhood fears had merged into one bizarre form.

"But they didn't quite work," she added. "I mean, there were traces of all the things I was scared of as a kid. But the face kept flowing, as if it couldn't make up its mind what it wanted to be. Does that make sense?"

Frankie shrugged, meditatively drying a plate while looking out at the sunlight garden. Finally, she spoke.

"A shrink would say you went to sleep in a strange place, just after having a disturbing experience thanks to Brie. So, your subconscious dredged up a whole lot of boogeymen, basically because everyone's subconscious is a total jerk."

Denny couldn't help laughing at Frankie's analysis, but felt herself agreeing with the gist of it.

"Maybe I should talk to Brie?" she suggested, as they finished putting away the crockery. "She can't sleep all day; we need to get ready for the big opening."

Frankie looked dubious.

"I reckon the big opening will be a bust," she said. "These things always are. The bigger the buildup, the bigger the letdown. Remember that old lumber mill in Maine?"

"Don't remind me!" replied Denny, shaking her head. "Believe me, I don't want to fall flat on my ass again. But we've got to have some gimmick for the show. 'Hey, we're spending the night in a haunted house' just won't cut it. Even if the house happens to be in England. We need to open that doorway."

They agreed to meet up outside the temple entrance later, then Frankie went to start setting up small cameras around the house. Activated by motion sensors, the cameras were standard equipment for the show.

Denny took a breath and paused outside the door of the dining room, listening. There was no sound from inside. She knocked gently on the dark wood panels, but there was no response from Brie. It occurred to Denny that the psychic might have simply gone upstairs to her new bedroom, while the rest of them were elsewhere. The kitchen was in back of the house, well away from the entrance hall.

"Brie?" she said quietly, opening the door a couple of inches. "You in there? Is it okay if I come in?"

There was a vague noise, somewhere between a moan and a grunt. The heavy curtains of the grand chamber had been drawn. A little light made it through chinks at the edges of the drapes. Denny crept inside, closing the door behind her, and waited for her eyes to adjust to the gloom. When she could see more clearly, Denny could make out a humped form on the sofa. Brie was evidently still asleep, covered with a tartan blanket. Denny went to stand over her colleague, unwilling to wake her.

"Brie?" she said.

When there was still no response Denny turned to leave.

"What?"

The voice was low, rasping, and Denny felt a pang of compassion for Brie. Looking closer, she saw that nothing of the woman's head showed except a few strands of fair hair.

She's been crying, maybe lost her voice. Not good for the show.

"Brie, I just wanted to check if you're okay?"

"I'm okay."

Again, the words were at a level just above a whisper. Denny bent down so she could hear Brie clearly.

"Can I get you anything? Coffee, or maybe a sandwich?"

"No," came the reply.

After hesitating a moment, Denny perched on the arm of the sofa and thought about how to discuss her own experience without alarming the other woman. They had never become friends, despite working together. Their relationship was purely work-based.

Partly my fault, Denny thought. *I focus on the job too much.*

"Brie," she said. "I had this—thing happen. In my room. I mean, in your old room. I saw something."

There was no response from the huddled figure below her. Then came a slight movement of the chunk of hair.

"What did you see?"

Denny tried to explain, recounting her experience as she recalled it, aware that she sounded very much like a child confusing a nightmare with reality.

"So," she concluded, "they searched the room but nobody found anything. I guess that means there was nothing there? Right?"

"Could go somewhere else," came the croaky response. "Big house."

It was a simple point, but one that Denny had not really considered. If what she had seen was a living entity—as opposed to an apparition—it could indeed have left the bedroom and gone into hiding elsewhere. There were dozens of empty rooms in Malpas Abbey. The weird being could be in any one of them, or in the attic.

"Good point, yeah," she breathed, not feeling very grateful to Brie for the worrying notion. Then, remembering what her colleague had been through, she went on, "Oh, I nearly forgot! Will you be able to take part? In the doorway sequence? Because we can only do it once."

Another pause, and Denny was about to repeat her question when the tress of hair moved again.

"I'll be there."

"Okay," said Denny, trying to sound bright and positive. "Looking forward to it. Remember, if you need anything, just holler."

She reached down to pat Brie's shoulder, but when her fingers brushed the woolen blanket, the body underneath jerked. Denny snatched her hand back.

"Sorry," she said.

As she left the dining room, she recalled how into hugs Brie had always been, sometimes to the point of annoyance.

Now she can't bear to be touched, thought Denny. *Whatever it was, it shook her up very badly.*

***

"All I'm saying is, if you're doing this, stop it."

Matt McKay stood, arms crossed, blocking Ted Gould's way out of the walled herb garden. The Englishman held out his hands in a placatory gesture.

"I'm not *doing* anything, Matt," Gould insisted. "I couldn't concoct an apparition of the sort those young ladies said they saw, even if I wanted to."

Matt looked skeptical.

"I don't like people on my team getting terrified, especially if it's happening off camera," he said. "And you and Jim—you've had plenty of time to prepare a few little tricks, right?

"Interesting that you would be happier if your people were terrified on camera," commented Gould. "But we're not here to scare anyone. We're here to conduct an investigation. Jim is as honest as the day is long, incidentally. That's why he was chosen to help out. He's reliable. Now, if you'll excuse me—"

Gould tried to step around Matt, but the younger man blocked his way back into the house.

"An investigation?" said Matt. "One your fancy foundation could easily have done without our help. So, what's the real motive here? Why us?"

Gould sighed.

"Because, despite whatever you may think, I believe that your team contains at least one genuine psychic. Someone who can somehow connect with—"

"With what?" Matt demanded. "Why do you never just spit it out and say ghosts, the afterlife, spirits of the dead? Isn't that what you're all about?"

Gould shook his head, then pointed down at the rich growth of weeds around them.

"No, Matt, that's not what I'm about. It's not death I'm interested in... it's life. Life as real in its way as any of those wild plants. A form of life that, like a weed, takes root where it can in our world. But not life as we know it."

Genuinely puzzled, Matt could only stare as Gould stepped around him.

"Do you mean aliens?" asked Matt, belatedly.

"Oh no," Gould replied. "If only it were that simple. But we are talking about beings from another world, if that's any help."

Matt was left staring at the door as it closed behind the

Englishman.

***

Despite her earlier scare, Denny managed to get a couple of hours sleep in the big master bedroom. She was woken by her cell phone's alarm just as the September sun was nearing the horizon, turning the sky myriad shades of red, orange, and gold.

This really is a beautiful place, she thought, as she freshened up. *Guess I'm lucky to be a part of this—whatever it is. Adventure? Yeah, let's call it an adventure.*

When she went downstairs, the others had already assembled in the main hall, apart from Frankie and Matt, who were setting up the shot outside the sealed doorway. Denny was pleased to see that Brie was looking much better. The color had returned to her face, and she was chatting happily with Jim. Gould, now wearing a bulging backpack, was exchanging banter with Marvin. The two seemed to have hit it off, surprising Denny.

"Hi!" Denny said, approaching Brie and Jim. To Brie she added, "So, did you finally manage to get some sleep?"

"Yes," the medium replied with a smile. Denny was pleased to hear that Brie's voice showed no sign of hoarseness. "It was okay in your old room. Cozy. And I didn't really feel comfortable on that couch."

"Aw, sorry, I shouldn't have disturbed you," Denny said. "But hey, you bounced back, good for you!"

Brie looked puzzled at that remark. Denny was about to say that Brie had seemed pretty washed out when they had talked earlier. But Gould interrupted, clapping his hands.

"Are we ready to go, team?"

As they followed the Englishman Brie asked, "Did you disturb me? I really don't recall. As soon as I got into a proper bed I was out like a light, believe me!"

"No, I meant when we talked downstairs," Denny explained, but the puzzlement on the other woman's face left her floundering. "In the dining room?"

Maybe she was half asleep and just forgot our conversation, Denny thought as Brie continued to look vacant. Then a more worrying thought struck her. *Maybe it's the pills. Best not push it.*

"So, Jim," Denny said, changing the subject. "Our handyman ready to work up a sweat? Gonna take your shirt off, give us gals a thrill?"

"Oh God, don't," replied Jim in mock anguish. "If this goes wrong, I'm going to be a prize berk."

"Berk? Is that a British curse word?" asked Denny, saying with a joshing tone. "Should I avoid it if I get to meet royalty one day?"

"Erm, well, it's a bit naughty, but nothing compared to what some of them say, allegedly—" Jim began, clearly unwilling to explain.

"Can we get on, people? Time's wasting," shouted Matt as the group rounded a corner. They walked past the peculiar graffiti on the wall. Denny noticed that Brie did not look up at the words, hurrying ahead with her gaze fixed on the floor in front of her.

"I'm ready to go, guys," Denny said. Frankie, wearing huge noise-canceling headphones, swung the camera around and gave Denny a thumbs up.

"Ready when you are," Matt said from behind Frankie.

Like we need a director, Denny thought.

"Well, this is it," she said to the camera. "For the first time in decades someone is going to enter the secret temple of Lord George Blaisdell. What will we find inside? Evidence of Satanic rituals? Who knows! That's all part of the fun. But guys, if there's a sacrificial dagger, it's mine. I called it."

Denny stepped back, then raising her voice a little, said, "Take it away, Jim!"

Jim hefted the sledgehammer, and Denny realized that it was an awkward tool to swing in the narrow corridor. Fortunately, Jim managed to take a proper swing and hit the bricked-up doorway dead center. There was a loud crash, echoing through the house, and an eruption of dust. A couple of bricks had been knocked out. Everyone else retreated, covering their mouths, as the Englishman took a second swing. This time a dozen bricks gave way, and a dark hole, big enough for a man to squeeze through, appeared in the doorway.

Jim stepped back and they waited for the dust to settle. Then Frankie moved forward, shining her camera light into the gaping void.

"What can you see?" asked Denny.

"A whole lot of doodly squat," replied Frankie, cheerfully. Then she put a hand to her headphones. "Whoa! Got a lot of feedback, there. Probably not a ghost, though."

"Okay, guys," said Denny, "pick up your flashlights. Jim, if you'd do the honors."

"My pleasure," replied Jim, and stepped forward again to knock away the remaining brickwork. When the dust had cleared a second time, Frankie stepped back into the aperture to get first shots of the interior. The others picked up flashlights, provided by Gould, and prepared to enter.

As usual, Denny led the way. She picked her way over the small heap of rubble. She was standing at the top of a flight of stairs that led down into a circular chamber about thirty feet across. The stone roof was low, no more than eight feet high. Her flashlight was just powerful enough to show that the walls were decorated with murals of some kind. She could also see a bulky object in the middle of the room.

"I think we found the altar that naughty old lord used, guys," she said over her shoulder. "Looks pretty creepy."

Denny went down the stairs, making her way carefully. Frankie followed, then the rest, the beams of flashlights flickering over walls and the floor. There were a few scraps of debris on the stairs. Denny bent down to pick up an old, yellowed sheet of newsprint. It was dated 1919.

"Hey guys," she said, holding the front page up for the camera, "apparently the US government's going to outlaw alcohol. You think that may have some unexpected consequences?"

This produced a ripple of slightly nervous laughter. The group descended to the chamber floor, then stood hesitantly around the base of the stone stairway. Nobody seemed to want to venture into the middle of the room. Denny decided to take the initiative and went to examine the murals on the circular wall.

It only took her a few moments to realize that they couldn't show the acts depicted by Blaisdell's artist. The violence might have been acceptable on TV, but the explicit sexual acts certainly were not. She found herself struggling, in the poor light, to imagine just how some of the debauchery depicted could have been achieved in real life. Then, when she saw a particularly horrific scene, she found herself hoping they had never been tried.

"Whoa," Denny breathed, "those old-time aristocrats were something else. Gonna have to blur out a lot of this stuff, Frankie."

"What is all this junk?" asked Marvin, who had gone in the opposite direction to Denny. He crouched down, rummaged through a small heap of cardboard boxes, then held up a rectangular object. "Hey, look! I found a camera! Kind of dusty, but it's neat."

"You found an antique," put in Frankie. "That thing runs on clockwork. It's an old cine camera, sixteen millimeter, looks like. My grandpa had one, they're cool."

There was a brief discussion as to whether the camera had film in it. After examining it, Frankie pronounced that it did and Gould offered to get it processed if possible. He made a big deal of the Romola Foundation's 'excellent facilities'.

That would make a nice extra, thought Denny. *Assuming the film shows anything interesting. And not just close-ups of those murals. Or a crazy guy murdering two other guys and arranging their body parts around the place.*

"Ted?" Denny asked, focusing on the audience. "The last time this place was opened some real bad things happened, right?"

Gould nodded.

"They bricked it up again after the incident," he said. "Though whether that worked is a moot point. After all, two of us had paranormal experiences before we broke through."

"Yeah, if the altar is the source of whatever goes on here, bricking it up clearly doesn't work," said Marvin, gazing at the lump of stone with obvious distaste. "What a comforting thought!"

"Hey," Brie put in, pointing. "What are you up to, Ted? That's not a camera?"

The Englishman had produced a small box from his backpack. Attached to it by a cable was a plastic tube, which he began to wave around in front of him.

"It's just a basic Geiger counter," explained Gould, with a smile at the others' obvious puzzlement. "You've seen 'em in the movies. Well, in real life they're much the same. Point at things, wait for the clicking noise. If it makes a very loud sound, step away from the object."

The Englishman frowned, then, and jabbed at a button on the control box.

"Well, it *should* be making a slight clicking noise, except that today it doesn't seem to be working. Odd. It was fine when I tested it earlier. And this chamber is lined and floored with stone, which always has some trace levels of radioactive isotopes."

Frankie made a sad trombone sound. Denny, suppressing a giggle, asked Gould why radiation was an issue in any case.

"It's basic science to take as many measurements as possible, get plenty of data," he replied, waving the detector back and forth. "When the Victorians started looking into the paranormal, they were quick to use photography. It makes sense to employ more advanced detection equipment now that we have it, yes?"

"Maybe," chipped in Marvin, "but I can't imagine a ghost being radioactive—or are you seeking the spirit of Robert Oppenheimer?"

Gould gave a thin smile and set off back up the flight of stairs. Near the top, he stopped, held up the Geiger counter, and then operated a control. A series of clicks came from the gadget.

"Getting anything, Ted?" asked Denny.

"Yes, it started working," he said, and began to walk down into the cellar again. Then he stopped, frowning. "But now the damn thing's not registering at all."

"Piece of junk," remarked Frankie, "you should get a refund."

Gould nodded absently, peering at the device's controls.

"Or," he said, "there really is no background radiation at all in this chamber."

"Hey, that's a good thing, right?" said Denny. "I mean, 'cause radiation's generally a bad thing?"

"But it is a universal thing," said Frankie. "It's everywhere on earth, or under it, right?"

Gould said nothing, but began to walk around the room, still frowning at his gadget. Frankie, meanwhile, moved forward and began to film the supposed altar. Examining the stone more closely, Denny could see that it had been carved quite elaborately at some remote time. The images had almost worn away over the centuries, but she could still make out the rudimentary forms.

"Faces," she said. "This thing's covered in weird faces."

Behind her, someone was trying to stifle a scream.

"What is it, Brie?" asked Jim.

"Footprints!" Brie said, as Frankie swung round to focus on her. Brie was pointing at the floor, and Denny could make out some tracks in the dust. "These footprints aren't ours!"

"Do ghosts usually wear Nikes?" asked Denny.

She was hunkered down next to the supposed ghostly footprints, which seemed to go all the way round the altar stone.

"Those tracks do look awful familiar," Frankie said. "And there's no way they were made back in 1919."

Denny stood up, turning to face the others.

"So, either it's ghosts with questionable fashion sense, or somebody here is messing with us."

Brie and Marvin looked startled, while Gould and Jim looked shifty. Matt, Denny noticed, was trying to move out of camera shot behind the bulk of Marvin.

"So, three of us were here first," Denny went on. "Preparing the ground, so to speak. Am I right, guys? What do you say, Ted?"

Gould folded his arms, trying to look unabashed.

"Yes, we did enter this chamber a few days ago," he said. "Just to make sure there was something here. It would have been embarrassing if it had been empty, after all."

Then Jim took a breath and spoke.

"We faked it," he said. "I knocked that wall down a couple of days ago. We had a look around, then I rebuilt it."

"It was part of our arrangement," put in Matt quickly. He looked around at his team defiantly. "Like Ted says, we had to be sure there was something to find! We couldn't come all this way for an empty cellar and a house that may be haunted."

"You jerks," said Frankie. "So that was all faked?"

Jim nodded.

"It's easy to dirty up the mortar," he explained. "In the poor light it looked like it hadn't been disturbed for years."

"But in fact," Gould said slowly, "there was a gap of around two hours when nobody was nearby and that doorway was open."

"Plenty of time for a whole army of little spooks to sneak out," remarked Marvin, with deceptive mildness. "Good job, guys."

"Frankie," said Matt, "please stop filming."

"Sure thing, boss!" Frankie's tone was fake-cheery.

"I'm sorry," said Brie, heading for the stairs. "I just can't go on with this—it's too much! I signed up for an entertainment show. All this fraud, on top of what I experienced. I quit! I need Jim to drive me back to town, whatever it's called."

"You're contracted to appear in the show," Matt pointed out, trying to head her off. "I sympathize, I really do. But a deal's a deal. Maybe you could just, you know, take another little rest? See how you feel later on?"

Crappy behavior, even for you, Denny thought. *You're not taking this place seriously enough.*

The team followed Brie up out of the cellar. The psychic was still demanding to leave and stay in a hotel or B&B in Chester. In the past, when Brie had had a bad reaction to a location, Denny and Frankie worked to talk her down. Now neither of them even tried.

"I'm sorry," repeated Brie. "It's just those faces on that altar reminded me of the thing I saw—the proportions were wrong, it looked inhuman. And this whole place, it's evil. I can sense it. And something else. Can't any of you feel it?"

"We've all seen the murals, honey," Marvin said, in his usual supercilious tone. "Clearly we are not in Disney World."

Brie shot him a hurt look, at which Marvin rolled his eyes.

"That's not what I meant!" Brie snapped. "I get this crawling sensation, like you get when someone's looking at you from behind. It's always there. Something's paying attention."

"It's only Jim looking at your ass," Marvin muttered. Denny quickly intervened to try and head off any pointless bickering.

"Maybe you could tell us what scared you when you were upstairs?" she asked Brie, gesturing at Frankie to get a medium close-up. "If you feel capable, that is. Talking about it some more might help."

Brie glanced at the camera for a moment, then back at the entrance to the underground chamber.

"I... I saw something scary in my room," she said after a moment's hesitation. "I'm not sure what it was. It had a weird face, deformed, freakish. I don't want to think about it at all. I just want to leave this place. Now. Please."

"Brie," said Gould, "would it help if I told you the whole truth about my own experience? The one I... I glossed over earlier?"

Brie looked uncertain but did not reject the idea out of hand.

"I knew it was bullshit!" exclaimed Marvin, triumphantly.

"True, I lied earlier when I was interviewed," Gould admitted. "Or rather, I told a heavily-edited version of the truth. That story about getting lost in the woods. It wasn't that straightforward. Maybe it will put things in perspective if I tell you what really happened—and what I discovered much later."

He paused, then looked Brie in the eye.

"We call what you saw an *Interloper*."

CHAPTER 4

LITTLE GIRL LOST

"Okay, so what did happen in that forest?" asked Denny.

Around the big kitchen table, the various team members looked on expectantly. Matt seemed angry at Gould for jeopardizing the show. Marvin had his characteristic half-smile of superiority. Brie was jittery, a mess of disordered hair and streaked mascara. Even Jim had lost his composure and glowered at his boss.

"If I tell you, promise you won't interrupt? I'm happy for Frankie to record this," he added. "People should know."

There were nods, noises of agreement. Frankie took out a small digital camera, began to film across the table. Gould sat back, looked into his coffee mug for a couple of seconds, then took a gulp. Another sigh, then he looked over at Denny and began to talk.

"She was called Lucy," he said. "She was my little sister, a couple of years younger than me. Of course, when you're an eight-year-old boy, that age difference can seem enormous. And my friends and I found her to be a terrific nuisance, always following us around. We had what we considered to be a gang, you see. We were the cool kids, and she was spoiling it, a little girl following boys around and wanting to join in with our games. It was particularly galling for me, of course—I was responsible for her. My parents made clear that I should always look out for Lucy. And naturally I didn't want to."

Gould paused then looked away, out of the kitchen window into the pitch darkness.

"And then one day I decided to play a nasty little prank."

***

"We've never come this far before," said Martin. "There's supposed to be an old well."

"My uncle said it's an abandoned mine shaft," interrupted Paul. "He said it's all overgrown and not properly fenced off."

"The point is," said Martin, sounding peeved, "that we're not supposed to go out of sight of the village."

Edward felt rising anger. His friends had complained incessantly about Lucy following them around. Now he had a plan to deal with it, and instead of doing as they were told, they were whining.

"I thought we didn't want girls in the gang?" Edward said, putting as much sarcasm into his tone as he could manage. "You two should be wearing frocks. With ribbons in your hair."

Martin's freckled face reddened, while Paul started to stammer—sure signs that Edward's insult had struck home. He pointed back along the forest trail at the tiny figure in red that was scampering through the autumn leaves. He could just make out Lucy's voice, plaintively shouting.

"Slow down, Edward! I'll tell Mummy!"

Always whining, he thought. *She never shuts up. Never leaves me alone.*

"Guys, you want to play with Lucy every weekend?" Edward demanded.

The other two shook their heads.

"Right," Edward went on. "So, let's give her a scare. Operation Little Red Riding Hood is under way."

Edward signaled to Paul, who nodded and stepped off the trail and behind a gnarled old elm. As he moved out of Lucy's line of sight, Paul opened his backpack and took out a Halloween mask. It was Dracula, complete with dripping fangs. Edward would have preferred something more disturbing, but they had had to work with what they could get in the village shop.

Besides, he thought, *Lucy is a real scaredy-cat.*

While Paul moved off into the undergrowth, Edward and Martin stood waiting for the little girl. Lucy was almost out of breath by the time she reached them, but she still had sufficient energy to pound her little fists on Edward's chest.

"I'm telling Mummy on you!" she exclaimed, in an irate squeak.

Grabbing his sister's wrists, Edward made placatory noises.

"Calm down, Luce! We were just messing around."

Lucy did not show any signs of letting her big brother off the hook and resorted to kicking him in the shins. Edward gave Martin a significant look. Martin rolled his eyes, then stepped forward and patted Lucy gently on the shoulder of her red duffel coat.

"There, there," said Martin, awkwardly. "We're both sorry."

Lucy snorted, but stopped kicking Edward, who made a mental note to call Martin 'Lucy's boyfriend' for the rest of the weekend. The little girl pouted up at Martin, who was notoriously soft-hearted and an easy target for Lucy.

"Hey," said Edward, trying to deflect her attention, "we're playing a game of hide and seek. Do you want to join in?"

Lucy looked dubious.

"We shouldn't be in the forest," she said sulkily. "You know Mummy said we shouldn't go inside."

"Oh, rules are made to be broken," said Edward breezily. He had just learned the phrase and liked to use it whenever he could. "We can have more fun playing hide and seek where there are lots of places to hide. Can't we?"

Lucy looked from her brother to Martin, who nodded encouragingly.

"All right," she said. "At least hide and seek is better than pretending to be soldiers. That's so boring."

Typical girl, thought Edward. *No idea how to have fun.*

"Paul's already gone to hide," explained Martin, pointing in the direction their friend had gone. "All we have to do is go and look for him."

Lucy nodded solemnly but made no move to step off the trail.

"We have to split up to search better," added Edward.

At that, Lucy began to pout again. She clearly suspected something, and for a second Edward thought their scheme was going fail before it had properly begun. But then Martin rescued the situation.

"And there's a special prize for the first person to find Paul," he said. "Chocolate! Just catch Paul and he'll give you a bar of Cadbury's Fruit and Nuts."

Lucy's eyes widened. She had a well-defined set of values, with candy of all kinds very near the top. After a moment's contemplation she smiled, and with a cheerful 'Okay!' set off into the undergrowth. As the little red figure vanished into the wild greenery, Martin and Edward took out their own masks—Frankenstein and a Mummy—and set off slowly after Lucy.

***

"Wow!" exclaimed Frankie. "You were a real Grade A douche, Ted!"

Denny silently concurred, but then felt guilty. The expression on Gould's face told its own story. The pain he felt was that of a raw wound, not some half-forgotten trauma he had come to terms with. Again, the Englishman scratched at the pale scar, half-hidden by his shirt sleeve.

"Kids don't always think about consequences," said Brie quietly. "We all did dumb stuff when we were small."

Gould gave Brie a faint smile.

"I tell myself that," he murmured. "But it's a flimsy excuse. I knew we were doing something bad, but I did it just the same. Organized it, persuaded the others to carry it through. I was quite simply a cruel, selfish little turd."

That silenced the rest of the group. Gould folded his hands and, again gazing out into the night, resumed his story.

"It was a stupid idea and it all went wrong, of course," he said. "But not in the way any of us could have predicted."

***

Edward realized the flaw in his plan half a minute after they had set off in pursuit of Lucy. The girl was too small and the woods too dense. Sneaking up on her and giving her a scare necessitated knowing where she was. Edward and Martin had spread out until they were about twenty yards apart. They tried to signal with gestures, but it was getting harder to see each other. It was mid-afternoon in October, and there was still enough foliage on the trees to block much of the slanting sunlight. Also, they were trying to move stealthily, and that slowed them down. There was no sign of Lucy and no sounds. Edward had expected his sister to thrash her way noisily through the under-brush. But everything was silent except for the occasional bird call.

What if she has an accident?

The thought struck Edward like a blow in the pit of his stomach. He had never taken his parents' warnings about the forest seriously. It was just a big clump of trees between his house and the village. The grown-ups were close-mouthed and vague about why the area was shunned. But the more he thought about Lucy picking her way through the darkening forest floor, the more he wondered about the mine shaft, or the well, or whatever danger might be hidden amid the greenery.

The scream was shocking, cutting through the cool air and making Edward jump. It was so piercing that for a moment he doubted if it could be Lucy. Then he sighed with relief.

Paul found her. He jumped out at her, gave her a scare. She's probably wet her knickers!

Edward smiled at the thought and started to move more quickly. The scream had come from somewhere ahead of him. He took off his mask, hid it in his bag, and began to shout Lucy's name. The plan was to make her believe there were monsters in the forest so that she would never come back. The scream, Edward reflected, sounded promising.

She'll be having nightmares until Christmas, he thought, with grim satisfaction. *If it keeps her away from us, it'll be worth a punishment from Dad.*

The second scream was fainter but drawn out for longer. It was worse, somehow. The first time had sounded right to Edward—the reaction of a silly girl surprised by a plastic mask. But why would Paul continue to torment Lucy?

Unless it's someone else.

Again, assorted grown-ups' warnings came to mind, swirling around his head as he began to stumble in a half run over the uneven ground. This time it was not the risk of accidents in the forest, but something even worse. The sort of thing that parents talk about in low voices after they've switched over in the middle of the news.

Don't talk to strangers. Never go anywhere with somebody you don't know. Never accept sweets. Even if someone says they know your mother or father, don't go with them.

"Oh God, please don't let it—" he gasped in an attempt at a prayer. "Please God, let her be all right. I'm sorry I did it, I didn't mean—"

Lucy's voice, plaintive now, sounded from somewhere ahead of him.

"Edward! Help!"

The brushwood grew denser, fallen branches, drifts of dead leaves, and dense clumps of weed all hindering his progress. It seemed to grow darker with each passing moment, now, and he told himself it was because a cloud had passed in front of the sun. Then he burst out of the undergrowth into a circular area about twenty yards across. It was thick with weeds but there were no trees, not even saplings. In the center of the clearing was a light-colored stone about five feet tall. It was lumpy, squat, somehow menacing.

Edward stopped in surprise. He had had no idea the clearing existed. The stone looked as if it had once been a statue of some kind, but almost all the carving had worn away, reminding him of the ancient gargoyles on the village church. It was, he realized, in the heart of the forest. He did not need to think about its significance. Edward knew, with terrible finality, that this was what people really feared about the forest. He felt a sudden urge to run away.

"Leave me alone!"

Lucy's voice came from the other side of the pale stone. Edward dashed around the stone and stopped, more astonished than scared by what he saw. Lucy was being dragged into a hole in the air. He saw her legs kicking out. One of her little black shoes was missing. The lower part of her red coat was visible, but not the rest of her. Lucy's upper body was invisible. But Edward could still hear her voice, screaming for help, but faintly as if she was at a great distance.

"Lucy!"

He ran forward and grabbed her legs, began to pull her out of the impossible aperture. As he struggled to save Lucy, part of Edward's mind registered that the 'hole' was a kind of foggy sphere, a region of air that shimmered like a heat-haze despite the cool October day. It was about four feet across, but its edges were hard to make out.

Edward did not try to make sense of it all. All he simply knew was that Lucy was vanishing, that it was somehow his fault for being mean to her, and that he had to save her. He dug in his heels and pulled harder. After a couple of seconds, Lucy came unstuck and was released, then he fell backwards. He fell against the white stone, and it winded him. Lucy dropped out of the air into a patch of wildflowers, her face pale, eyes staring, but apparently unhurt.

As soon as she focused on Edward, she jumped up and flung herself on him. She did not cry, simply clung to him. Her utter stillness scared him even more than her screams had done. He saw red welts on her arm, felt terrible shame at his part in what was happening.

"It's all right," he said, trying to convince them both. "It's all right, we're going home now, Lucy."

He staggered to his feet, tried to set his sister down, but she was determined to cling to him with arms and legs. Rather than argue with the terrified girl he turned to leave the clearing via the rough trail he had forged.

"Hurry," he heard her say into his shoulder. "She's coming!"

Edward wanted to ask who she meant, but before he could ask, he felt a blow in the middle of his back. He fell forward, heavily, crushing Lucy underneath him. The girl's screams blended with another sound, a kind of low snarling and hissing. Sudden, intense pain shot through his back. He felt his shirt rip, and his flesh. Edward screamed, rolled over, punched and kicked blindly at his assailant. His fist connected with a face that he could just make out in the gloom. The figure crouching above them jumped up, making a kind of mewing noise.

I hurt it, he thought. *And it's not very big.*

Then another figure appeared, and a third. They leaped at him, their hands making the slashing motions he had seen in fighting cats. They were all child-sized, but fast-moving and disturbingly strong. Their faces were hard to make out, especially as they darted and lunged at him. Edward raised his hands in front of his face, and a burning pain shot through one forearm.

Two of the creatures were keeping him occupied, while the third dragged the screaming Lucy back towards the shimmering, cloudy sphere. No matter how much Edward tried, he couldn't get to her. Then the sky must have cleared, and a shaft of sunlight lit up the clearing. The golden glow caught one of the monsters on the face, and Edward reeled back, almost falling, hands raised now not to ward off attack but to block a horrific, impossible sight.

The thing had Lucy's face, but the features were not quite finished. The snub nose seemed half-melted, like candle wax, the mouth was little more than a crude slit, the eyes small and beady. Yet the resemblance was still there in the shape of the face, the proportions of the small body. The hair that straggled from the nightmare being's head was the exact color of Lucy's auburn.

"You shouldn't be so nasty to me, Edward," lisped the half-formed mouth. "We're family, after all."

***

"The next thing I remember," said Gould, after a pause, "was running through the forest, shouting for help. Martin and Paul found me, and tried to calm me down, get me to explain. But I couldn't—I couldn't make sense out of what had happened. I just kept saying 'Lucy's gone, they stole her face'."

"Oh, my Lord," whispered Brie, eyes bugging. "The thing's face—like the one I saw. Not quite human, but so close it was horrible."

"I saw one, too," murmured Denny. "Complete with unfinished features. Maybe mine couldn't decide on a face."

Gould nodded, then reached into the jacket that he had hung on the back of his chair. He took out a flask and poured amber liquid into his coffee. He offered the flask around. Only Frankie took a mouthful, coughed. Denny caught the distinct odor of Scotch whiskey.

"Wow, that's the good stuff all right," she spluttered.

This prompted nervous laughter, and everyone started talking at once. Matt seemed to think the entire experience was a kind of false memory covering a more disturbing, but entirely natural, incident. Marvin dismissed that idea, while Denny tried to mediate. Frankie continued to film what became a heated discussion, while Gould sat looking into the distance, evidently wrapped up in his memories.

"Okay," said Matt loudly, holding up his hands for silence, "the stone in the forest, whatever it was. If people knew it was there, warned their kids not to go near it, why didn't they do something about it? Smash the stone, maybe concrete over the whole clearing. Hell, why not tell the police, MI5, whatever?"

"Good question," Gould conceded, absentmindedly running a finger along the scar on his forearm. "But many years later when I asked local people, including my parents, about the forest, none of them could say why it was reputedly a bad place. It just was. Nobody went there.

That was the key fact. Stories about a well, or an old mine, or lurking perverts were concocted after the fact. As for the stone, well, it was just a bit of old rock. For the authorities, there was nothing to connect it to a little girl vanishing."

Matt gave a noncommittal grunt.

"But you're right," Gould went on. "The police did investigate the whole area, and they did the clearing. There was no sign of a struggle, not a trace of Lucy. None of her clothes, or her shoes, were found. Not that day, at least. It was a mystery—made the national papers. The place was swarming with reporters."

The story isn't over, thought Denny. *That's why he needed a slug of whiskey. There's even worse to come.*

"I heard the story in fragments, down the years," Gould went on. "They sent me away to my grandparents for a fortnight after the disappearance. My physical injuries were treated, blamed on broken glass or wood splinters. I had no therapy, of course—I told you this happened a long time ago. Just a little holiday. So, I wasn't there when they found the body two days later. It was on the edge of the forest, the side nearest our house, not the village side. She was in her red coat, with her dress, socks, shoes—all readily identified. The only strange thing was that the dress was wrongly buttoned. And her shoes were on the wrong feet."

"You mean," gasped Brie, "someone had undressed her, then—Oh Lord."

Gould stared into his coffee for a long moment before resuming.

"In those days, of course, they did not have very advanced forensic techniques. Certain tests were made, and I later found out that an autopsy was carried out. The results were described as inconclusive, but heart failure during an assault was settled upon as the cause of death."

"And that was it?" asked Matt. "You were all very British about it, I guess?"

"I never talked to my father about it, if that's what you mean," replied Gould. "After we lost Lucy, something in him died. He carried on working, but everything else—he would just sit in front of the telly, only spoke if you talked to him. Eventually they separated, and my mother raised me. Sometimes bereavement does that—smashes a family apart."

There were sympathetic nods, and Matt seemed about to speak, then thought better of it. Denny recalled how needy and clingy he had been when they'd had their brief, unwise fling. Matt had lost his mother when he was young, she remembered. *I'm not here to psychoanalyze my co-workers, or ex-lovers,* she thought. Denny focused once more on what Gould was saying.

"I could almost have written off everything that happened in that clearing, if it had not been for my mother's attitude. My mother was stronger than us menfolk, I suppose. That's often the case. But she never discussed it, either. Once I caught her crying on Lucy's birthday, but that was it. Then my father died, still quite young, and at his funeral, my mother told me something. At first, I didn't understand what she had said, it was so unexpected."

Gould looked up at Denny, then at the others around the table.

"It wasn't her. That's what my mother said."

For a moment Denny was puzzled, then realized what Gould meant, given the context.

"It wasn't Lucy?" asked Brie, frowning. Then understanding dawned. "You mean they found—that creature?"

Gould nodded.

"It took a while for me to get the rest of the story out of her. She and my father had had to identify the body, you see. But when she saw it, she became convinced that it was not her daughter lying on the slab in the county mortuary. My father, at first, thought she was merely in shock. Then, as she continued to insist that Lucy was still alive, he became angry, confused, and unable to talk to her at all. From then on, they only communicated about mundane things, never really talked. And because I was a child, they didn't tell me."

"But isn't that called Impostor Syndrome?" asked Marvin. "When

72

people get the idea a loved one has been replaced by a lookalike, somehow? It's a mental disorder."

"True," said Gould. "But in Impostor Syndrome it's always a living relative, never a dead one. And there's more. Many years later, when I first became involved with the foundation, I sought out the doctor who had performed the postmortem examination. Turned out he'd retired."

***

"Dr. Beddows gets a bit confused," the nurse explained, leading Gould into the day room. It was a pleasant July morning and the residents of the Bide-a-Wee Home for Retired Gentlefolk were enjoying the sunshine. Two elderly men were playing chess, while a white-haired old lady was busy with the Times crossword. But about a dozen other old folk were simply basking in the golden light.

The nurse gestured at a man with a mop of gray hair and a straggling goatee sitting on his own in a wing-backed armchair. Gould went over and introduced himself, then tried to explain why he was there. But Beddows gave no sign that he recognized Lucy's name, staring up at Gould with watery, pale blue eyes.

"Michael?" the old man asked. "Is that you?"

"He thinks you're his son," the crossword lady explained. "Lives abroad, never visits. This often happens, I'm afraid. He has good days, but this might not be one of them."

Gould introduced himself and offered to shake Beddows' hand, but the old man just looked blankly up at him.

"I'm here to ask about Lucy, my sister," Gould said, speaking slowly. "She was found dead, and you examined her body. Do you remember that?"

"Lucy? No, no," said Beddows, shaking his head emphatically so that a cowlick of white hair flopped over his forehead. "No, you told me that your lady friend is called Carla. Or was it Martha?"

Gould pulled up a chair and tried to explain again, but Beddows just asked a series of questions about Michael's work and family life. They talked at cross-purposes for a couple of minutes, but it was clear that the old doctor was just becoming more agitated. Gould stood up, frustrated at hitting a blank wall in his investigation. At the same time, he felt sorry for Beddows, left to vegetate by his only close relative.

"I'm sorry, doctor," Gould said, offering his hand to the old man again. "I shouldn't have bothered you. I just wanted to know about Lucy."

"At first I felt bad because it was a child," murmured Beddows. "Then I felt frightened, because it was all wrong."

Gould stopped, and tried to process what he had just heard.

"The Lucy Gould autopsy?" he asked, sitting down again. "There was something wrong, something strange about it?"

"Everything was wrong—it was so disconcerting!"

Beddows was staring intently up at him now, his eyes focused, his manner showing no hint of confusion. The old man's gnarled hand fastened on Gould's arm, gripped it with surprising strength.

"It was almost a child, you see," he hissed. "Almost, but not quite. The organs weren't right, and the skeletal structure—everything was simplified, as if someone had taken tissue, bone, and cartilage to make a living doll, a passable facsimile. I remember thinking how awful if that creature had lived, passing for human, but not. Going to school, sitting at the dinner table, being tucked in bed. The brain was outlandish. What thoughts might such a thing have had?"

The old man shuddered. Gould struggled to process what he had just heard. The pleasant, sunlit room seemed impossibly calm and ordinary. Not a place for such revelations.

"You're sure it wasn't my sister?" he demanded, struggling to keep his voice low as the other residents looked on. "It wasn't Lucy at all?"

Beddows nodded gravely, then looked around.

"These people can't imagine it," he whispered. "The things I saw. Beneath the skin, so much that wasn't right. Monstrous! But who could I tell? I had a career, a position in the community. The newspapers had already reported the death of a child. The police had it all typed and filed. Terrible thing. Grieving parents. So, I signed the forms, wrote what they wanted, kept my nose clean. Oh yes. It had already begun to decay, you see. Disintegration accelerated rapidly once it set in. Soon there would be nothing identifiable!"

"You did what they wanted?" asked Gould, taking the old man's hand in his. "Who do you mean? Did someone pressure you?"

Beddows frowned. His expression of intense concentration faded, facial muscles slackening. The old man leaned back in his chair, which creaked.

"Pressure? No, no pressure at all—it's very relaxing here. Everyone is very kind. But I do get lonely, sometimes, Michael. I wish you'd come more often."

***

"Oh my God," said Denny. "That's horrible."

It's also ratings gold, she could not help thinking. *The guy's a natural storyteller.*

"It has the ring of truth," added Marvin, again surprising Denny.

He's given up on his trademark cynicism, she thought.

"But what are these things?" demanded Matt. "Where do they come from? Do you know, Ted? Don't hold out on us, not in this situation"

Gould rubbed his chin, glanced around at his listeners.

He's wondering how much more to reveal, thought Denny. *I'll bet our audience gets that.*

"Okay," Gould said. "The scientists I work with think the Interlopers come from what they've dubbed the Phantom Dimension. PD for short. A real, physical realm, like our own universe, but existing parallel to it. Obviously one world is closed off from the other, but there are weak spots where energy and matter can pass through. Gateways, if you like. Our ancestors knew about them and placed those odd marker stones to show where they could sometimes be found. I'm sure that some stones were simply warnings, like a buoy marking a wreck."

It took the others a few moments to process these ideas.

"So, the stones aren't sacrificial altars?" asked Marvin.

"Some might have been," admitted Gould. "We don't know, despite many decades of research. All over the world, you find stones carved with strange faces, not quite human visages. It's conventional to say the prehistoric cultures that produced them were depicting their gods, or demons. And that is what the Interlopers must have seemed, for a long time. Beings that could change their shape, appearance, and drag people into some strange realm. The Trickster of Native American myth, the Little People of Celtic folklore. There are lots of variations on the theme."

"These things are intelligent?" Denny asked.

Gould nodded emphatically.

"Intelligent, aggressive, cunning. And not bound by the same physical laws as ourselves. That's why they can read our thoughts, to some extent, and change their appearance accordingly. In the Phantom Dimension, what we call magic seems to prevail—willpower alters reality. It might be that that is where we get all our magical beliefs—half remembered stories about the PD and its denizens."

"Hang on," interrupted Matt. "If they enter our world, surely our laws apply?"

"That's a good point," agreed Gould. "Some believe there's a kind of conservation of energy involved—they can survive here for a while because they bring their own weird reality with them. But this power they have dwindles, is diluted by our reality, so that they must return to the PD or suffer dissolution. Like the Interloper that took Lucy's form— something went wrong, it died, and disintegrated."

"So, it decayed because it ran out of paranormal juice?" asked Marvin.

"You have a knack for making the most serious matter seem frivolous," replied Gould.

Soon everyone was talking at once, throwing questions at Gould, interrupting one another. Then Jim banged the flat of his hand down on the table. For the first time since Denny had met him, the stocky man looked angry. And scared.

"This is all very nice," Jim said. "But what I've heard only convinces me that we're in immediate danger. We should go. Now."

This triggered more argument, as the group split along predictable lines. Jim and Brie were keen to get out at once, while Gould and Matt both wanted to stay and finish filming. Marvin, Frankie, and Denny were caught in the middle.

It's a great opportunity to get rock-solid evidence of the paranormal, Denny thought. *But only if we live through it.*

"If we stick together," Gould was saying, "they can't do us any harm. Remember, they prey on our weaknesses; fears, hopes, deep emotions. A group is too diverse to attack in that way."

Jim began to protest, but Gould shut him down with a single remark.

"Are you quitting your job, Davison? Because I hear you ex-army types have poor employment prospects these days."

It's a stalemate, Denny thought. *But we came here to make a show.*

"Ted," she said, "if we filmed the gateway to this other dimension that would be the clincher. So far we've got nothing useful on tape."

"If we got that, we could leave," conceded Matt. "So, we go back into that temple, see what happens, right?"

"No," said Brie. "Everything Ted has said just convinces me I need to get far away from this place. I still want to leave!"

CHAPTER 5

LITTLE BOY LOST

"Okay," said Denny, trying to salvage something before they had to stop filming. "Maybe you guys could tell us something about the psychic aura of this—whatever it is, altar?"

Marvin snorted in derision.

"Down there is just some dirty minded old lord's rumpus room," he said, gesturing at the doorway. "I sense a lot of tension, fear, confusion—but only from the living people standing right here. There are no spirits, evil or otherwise."

"But Brie says she can sense evil," Denny objected. "So, who's right? Ted? Do you feel anything?"

Gould shook his head.

"Apart from a chill, no. And I don't claim to be psychic. Anyway, the cold is what you'd expect in an unheated cellar in autumn."

"I want to go now," Brie insisted. "I will not spend the night here. Will somebody call me a taxi? Or should I do it myself?"

"Okay," Denny sighed, looking into the camera. "For the first time in the history of 'America's Weirdest Hauntings', one of the team has—let's say—withdrawn from the field of battle."

Brie really is freaking out, she thought. *And I don't blame her. If what she experienced was worse than my encounter, she's right to draw the line.*

After Frankie had stopped filming, Gould arranged for Jim to take Brie into Chester and find her someplace to stay. Brie also insisted that Jim come upstairs with her so she wouldn't be alone while she packed. The rest of the team adjourned to the kitchen, where an old kitchen range provided much needed warmth.

"Guess we can film them driving away," Matt said, sulkily. "Or can we simply edit Brie out?"

Denny began to protest, but Frankie settled the issue by pointing out that they already had several hours of footage that included Brie.

"Crap," said Matt. "We'd have to miss out all the preparations back in the States, the flight, arriving in England."

"Can't be done," Frankie said, with finality. "Make a virtue of necessity, play up why she's leaving."

"Prescription meds?" Marvin asked in his all-too-familiar bitchy tone.

Gould looked startled at this but said nothing. Matt shot Marvin a 'cut it out!' look.

"Okay, I'm not on any kind of pills, and I'm still pretty sure I saw something," insisted Denny. "Maybe not a ghost, or the devil, but something scary and weird. This house is haunted in some way."

"But we've got nothing on tape!" said Matt, frustration clear in his voice. "Two of the team are confronted by God-knows-what, and they're alone with no camera running."

"Maybe that's it," said Denny. "Whatever we're dealing with doesn't show itself to more than one person. Perhaps it preys on *individual* fears somehow? What do you think, Ted?"

Gould looked cagey, then shook his head.

"In the past, more than one person has been involved in manifestations," he pointed out. "And in 1919, something supposedly killed or wounded several people."

"Or they went crazy and attacked each other," Matt said. "That was the official verdict, wasn't it?"

"Yes," Gould admitted. "But when you consider the evidence..."

The debate went to and fro until they were interrupted by a text message from Brie to Denny, 'Ready to go!' When they got to the main hall, she was descending the stairs, followed by Jim, who was loaded down with her luggage. Denny again tried to persuade Brie to stay but failed. When Jim opened the front door, a gust of chill, damp night air blew in. It was now pitch dark outside.

No streetlights, thought Denny, with a shiver. *We're a long way from help.*

"Well, if you have to go, good luck," she told Brie. "And don't keep Jim to yourself, we need him here."

Brie said her slightly awkward farewells then left, clutching Jim's arm as he struggled with her bags. Matt shut the front door behind them and as he did, the hall lights flickered, died, then came on again.

"Looks like she left just in time," observed Marvin, wryly.

"It's probably just the old wiring," said Gould, but without much conviction.

"First that thing with the Geiger counter, now this," Denny said. "Any connection, Ted?"

"Electrical equipment sometimes becomes unreliable in these situations," replied the Englishman. "But you all knew that already, I'm sure?"

True, Denny thought, *but why do I get the feeling you know a lot more than you're letting on?*

Matt, Denny, and Frankie began to discuss how they would cope if the power failed. They had batteries for most of their equipment, but recharging might become an issue if they had no power for the whole night. Frankie decided to start the raw editing process, beginning with footage from the various automatic cameras.

"So, I put one camera in the hall," she said, "looking down from above the doorway, right? So here's Brie after her panic, going into the dining room for a lie down, Jim and me take her inside, then you see us come out."

"Okay," said Denny, "you know the motion sensor thingy works. So what?"

"So, this," Frankie said, as the others gathered around the kitchen table to look at the laptop screen. "See, this is Brie leaving the dining room to go upstairs, just a few minutes later. Now we jump forward about ten minutes and this is you, see?"

Denny stared, confounded by what she was seeing. She watched herself knock gently on the dining room door, then go inside. Frankie skipped forward a few minutes and Denny emerged, closing the door gently behind her. Another fast forward and the team gathered in the hall, Brie descending the stairs, followed a couple of minutes later by Denny.

"Oh my God," Denny breathed.

"I don't get it," said Matt. "So, you went into an empty room and came out again? We're not making art-house movies, guys."

"I talked to Brie in there," Denny said, looking at Matt, then Gould, then back at Frankie. "She was curled up on the couch under a rug. I heard her speak!"

But I never saw her face, she thought. *Or even the slightest bit of her skin. Just that hunk of hair.*

"But nobody else went into the room," Gould pointed out. "Or left it. Did they?"

"Good point!" Frankie murmured. "Let's just check."

She reversed the video slowly. It jumped from the point when the camera detected Denny to Brie going upstairs. Frankie slowed things down even more and began to inspect the movie one frame at a time.

"There," she said, freezing the image and pointing at the screen. "See? Something there."

Brie was just vanishing upstairs. Behind her, a blurred shape was emerging from one of the many anonymous corridors of Malpas Abbey. It was out of focus, so that Denny could only just make out a form that was vaguely human in shape. The next frame was time-stamped much later, and showed Denny coming from the kitchen into the hall.

"The motion sensor had trouble with it," Frankie said. "Like your Geiger counter, maybe, Ted? Something about these boogeymen screws up our tech. But it's there. The little gadget that caught something."

Open-mouthed, Denny looked up from the screen to see Matt giving her a mirthless grin, while Gould looked more thoughtful.

"It seems you actually conversed with some kind of entity," said

Gould.

"And you didn't notice," added Marvin, stroking his chin. "Not sure what that says about you. Or Brie, for that matter."

"Close encounter, girlfriend," said Frankie.

***

"I'm so grateful," said Brie, as Jim helped load her bags into the SUV. "I just want to get home to my boys, you know? I've never been so far away from Tommy—that's my son. I never thought I could miss someone so much."

She's yearning for familiar surroundings, Jim thought. *Figures. If I was half a world away from home and terrified out of my wits, I suppose I'd be the same.*

"No problem," the Englishman replied. He could just make her out in the light spilling from the round window above the front door. Rain was falling, and Jim wished he had put on a thicker coat. But he had assumed he would be spending most of this assignment indoors.

"Okay, Brie," he said cheerfully, as he slammed the rear door of the Mercedes. "Let's get you back to civilization. Well, Chester at least. Near as, makes no difference!"

They got into the car and buckled up. Jim was about to start the engine when he paused. He had glimpsed movement through the rain-spattered windshield. A pale object, low on the ground.

Furtive, Jim thought. *Skulking. Lurking on the edge of visibility.*

"Is something wrong?" Brie asked, her voice betraying jangled nerves.

Get a grip, he told himself. *This woman is on edge, she doesn't need any more scares.*

"No, nothing!" he said. "Thought I saw a deer, that's all. Or maybe it was a badger. Lots of wildlife out here."

Jim started the engine and began to maneuver the vehicle carefully down the rutted driveway towards the main gate. The wipers and headlights seemed oddly ineffective, and he struggled to make out anything ahead of them. Then the white pillars loomed up and he heaved a sigh of relief.

"Not far to the main road," he said. "Then it's a straight drive into Chester and we can—"

A sudden shock ran through the car, which lurched to one side. Brie screamed as Jim struggled to control the big Mercedes, but it slewed off the road and collided with a granite gatepost. There was a sickening crunch, and the engine died.

"Damn it! We blew a tire!"

"Oh, God," said Brie. "This damned place! It's not going to let me get away!"

Jim reassured her that it was just an accident, probably down to a piece of broken glass, and he could change the tire easily enough. He tried to speak with more confidence than he felt. He had checked out the driveway himself a couple of days earlier. It had been in poor condition, but there had been no glass or other hazards.

"Okay, you stay here with the heating on," he said, restarting the engine. "I'll get out and fix the tire. If I can't fix it, we can just walk back up to the house and take Ted's car, see? No problem."

Brie whimpered a little but did not protest as Jim got out a flashlight. When he stepped out into the darkness, the chill struck him again. The rain had already turned the dirt underfoot to mud, and for good measure, he had driven them into a patch of waist-high nettles that stung his hands as he worked. Cursing under his breath, Jim got the tools and began to jack up the vehicle. When he removed the front wheel, he gave the blown tire a cursory examination. It was hard to tell in the poor light what had caused it to fail.

Looks like it was slashed, he thought, running a finger along a tear in the rubber. *Cut deep, but not right through. Just enough so it would run for a few minutes before blowing. Is someone pranking us?*

Jim glanced around, swinging his flashlight. The beam showed raindrops, damp nettles, muddy ground, and gravel. He shone the flashlight up at the gatepost, squinting as it illuminated a grotesque statue squatting on top of the pillar. It was gargoyle-like, a grotesque diminutive figure squatting above him. Lit from below, it seemed doubly uncanny.

Like a gargoyle on an old church. But at least a carving can't hurt you, he thought. *Whoever or whatever cut that tire, on the other hand…*

Shrugging off the thought, Jim resolved to be practical. He put the flashlight down and began to attach the spare wheel. More stings added to his frustration, and he wished he had some thick gloves. Still, he was making good progress. But as he worked, a nagging doubt began to worry at the back of his mind.

The gateposts, he thought. *Details are wrong, somehow.*

When he finished, he got the flashlight and shone it up at the gatepost again. There was nothing on top of the pillar. He shone the flashlight over at the other gatepost. It was topped by a granite ball. Jim began to work frantically, kicking the jack away and not bothering to collect the tools. He snatched open the SUV's door. Brie stared into the flashlight beam, her eyes huge with fear.

"Okay," said Jim, trying not to sound overly concerned. "We're good to go."

"What's wrong?" Brie asked.

"Nothing," he said firmly, fumbling with his safety belt. "Got the wheel fixed, no problem."

He clashed the gears putting the Mercedes into reverse, then spun the wheels in the mud. The SUV backed up a few inches then slid forward, hitting the granite gatepost again. Jim took his foot off the gas, tried to gulp down his nervousness, tried again. This time the big car struggled back onto the furrowed driveway, slewing from side to side as Jim revved the motor.

"Right," he said, changing gear. "Let's get out of this godforsaken—"

The sound of the rain and wind grew suddenly louder. A chill blew through the interior of the SUV. In the rearview mirror, Jim saw a pale shape moving swiftly in the gloom as he heard one of the rear doors close. He lifted the flashlight as high as he could in the confined space, prepared to bring it down hard.

"What is it?" asked Brie, twisting around in her seat. "Did that thing get inside?"

"Don't worry," he said. "I'll sort it out. Just get ready to run if—"

"Mommy?"

The voice was that of a child. Jim hesitated, lifted himself in the seat to look into the back of the Mercedes. He could just make out a pale face looking up at him. It was apparently that of a small boy, small features topped by a mop of brown hair. Definitely not the leering gargoyle figure he had seen earlier.

"What are you doing here?" he asked, turning the flashlight to illuminate the newcomer. Small, skinny hands quickly covered the face.

"Mommy! The light's too bright!"

An American accent, Jim thought, brain racing.

"Tommy?" said Brie, unfastening her seat belt. "Is that you?"

"Mommy!"

The small figure flung itself forward between the seats, and wrapped pale, skinny arms around Brie. Jim saw then that the diminutive figure was clad in some kind of grayish-brown, ragged garment, more like some kind of medieval robe than regular clothes.

"Who is this?" Jim demanded. "Brie?"

"It's Tommy! Can't you see?" Brie looked at him over the small head she was clutching to her. "Jim, this is my son!"

"It can't be!" Jim protested. "How did he get here all the way from America?"

"The bad people brought me," said the boy, speaking in muffled tones. His head turned, and he looked at Jim. In the beam from the flashlight, the being Brie insisted was Tommy did look like a normal child.

There's definitely a family resemblance, Jim thought. *The nose, and the eyes.*

"Who brought you?" he asked. "Who are the bad people?"

"You are!" yelled 'Tommy', then buried his face in the front of Brie's coat again. Jim hesitated, wondering if he should continue with their journey or turn back.

This is just the sort of thing Gould needs to know about, he thought.

"Does it matter how he got here?" Brie demanded, her voice quavering with emotion. "He's scared! We've got to go! Get him to safety!"

"Okay," said Jim, shrugging. He put the Mercedes into gear and nosed it through the gate. But as the road came into view in the headlights, Tommy began to thrash around and whine.

"No, no, don't take me away!" he cried. "Take me back to the big house!"

For the first time since the newcomer had appeared, Brie looked uncertain.

"No, honey," she said, "that's a bad place."

"That's not your son!" Jim shouted, his mind suddenly clear of all doubt. "It makes no sense, Brie!"

"Tommy?" breathed Brie. Jim pulled up and again raised the heavy flashlight, but hesitated to bring it down on what still looked very much like a child's head. Tommy had become very still, his arms still wrapped around Brie. Then he emitted a growling noise that sounded more like a vicious dog than a child.

"No!" Brie shouted, trying to push the creature away. In a matter of seconds, Tommy had started to change, limbs growing longer and thinner, head losing its human-like roundness, hair becoming more sparse. The creature suddenly darted its head up and fastened onto Brie's face. Jim heard a sickening sound, part biting, part suction. Brie screamed and thrashed, trying to break free of the monstrous embrace, as Jim brought the flashlight down hard on the back of the elongated head. The being emitted a snarl, twisted its head around a hundred and eighty degrees, revealing a blood-stained muzzle.

Part-wolf, part-baboon, thought Jim, as he aimed another blow. Even as he brought his improvised club down, the creature was lunging toward him and the blow barely connected with the white, bare shoulder. The creature shoved its inhuman face towards Jim's, and he glimpsed an array of needle-like, blood-stained teeth. Impeded by his safety belt, Jim tried to grab his assailant by its long neck, but it was too fast and too strong. He flinched, closing his eyes, trying to protect his face with his free hand. He felt pain and the hot gush of blood.

"Get out Brie!" he shouted. "Run!"

***

"Okay," said Matt. "So, what have we learned from this?"

"These things are way out of our league," said Denny. "I vote we quit."

"Seconded," said Frankie.

Matt and Gould both began to protest at the same time.

"Seriously?" Denny said, hands on hips. "This is not listening for things that go bump in the night, guys. We've never encountered anything this extreme."

"No," said Gould, "but you've come close to them a few times."

"What?" exclaimed Matt. "You never told me that!"

Denny and the rest of the 'America's Weirdest' team listened while Gould explained why the Romola Foundation had invited them to England. By the time he had finished, Matt was even madder about the information withheld, and other team members were not far behind.

"And you chose now to tell us?" shouted Denny. "Jesus!"

"I'm sorry," Gould said. "But if we had told you that one of your team has an affinity with these beings it would have tainted the experiment."

"Well, we wouldn't want that," said Marvin. "Anyone else feel like a rat in a maze?"

"Rest assured," Gould went on, "that anyone who wants to join Brie can do so. I'll drive you back to Chester myself."

"What if we all want to quit?" demanded Denny, angrily. "Because I've had enough of your bullshit, Ted."

"Hey, let's not be hasty!" Matt began but hesitated at a sound in the distance. "What was that?"

"The front door?" suggested Frankie. "Jim can't be back already?"

They had just reached the door into the hall when it was yanked open and Brie rushed through, colliding with Denny. Brie was bleeding from a cut on her cheek. Gould and Marvin held the psychic upright while she babbled about 'Tommy' and 'monsters'. Denny wrinkled her nose. Along with Brie came a stench, like rotting meat. Then Denny saw Jim coming through the front door, carrying something in his arms. It was a gray-brown, nondescript object wrapped in Jim's jacket. Denny saw that it was dripping an oily black fluid onto the floor tiles.

"It just died," said Jim flatly, throwing his burden down.

The stench grew stronger when the rotting creature hit the floor. The impact sounded to Denny like wet laundry being dropped. The group formed a semi-circle around the disparate jumble of organic debris, exclaiming at the foul odor. There was little to see apart from a spreading puddle of putrefaction. A few traces of what might have been bones, organs and tendons were rapidly disintegrating.

"What the hell is that?" asked Marvin, stepping away.

"It's an Interloper," said Gould, covering his mouth with a scarf. "I've never seen one this close. Not in a long while, anyway."

"You've even got a name for these things?" Jim said resentfully. "You might have given me a heads up, boss! It scared the crap out of us. It could have killed us both if it hadn't suddenly fallen apart. Brie's wound isn't too bad but it will need cleaning, can somebody see to that?"

"I'll do it," said Marvin.

To Denny's surprise, Marvin took Brie gently by the arm and led her to the kitchen, where they'd stowed their First-Aid kit.

"I'm sorry, everyone," said Gould, "but I never expected them to be so aggressive all at once. Normally they lurk on the margins of perception, observing. When they decide to meddle, though—"

"They kill people, or try to," said Jim. "Ted, I vote we all get out of here."

"Same here," Denny and Frankie said simultaneously.

"What I said earlier stands," Matt insisted. "We can't just walk away from here with nothing. We can't afford it."

Matt looked around at his team.

"If we don't get a usable show out of this, it's game over," he went on. "Ratings have not been great for the last season. If we go back empty handed, the network drops us, and we've got nothing."

"You kept this quiet!" objected Denny. "What happened to all that stuff about us being one big happy team?"

CHAPTER 6

THE EXCHANGE

After much bickering, it was decided that Jim would remain with Brie while the rest of the team filmed for an hour in the cellar. If nothing happened, they would leave. Matt was grumpy about the last point, arguing that they had nothing of value in the can.

"We've had real paranormal experiences," Denny pointed out. "And two of us were attacked, could have been killed. What more do you want?"

Gould tried and failed to persuade Marvin to come with them, arguing that a psychic would be useful.

"I'm happy here," Marvin said. "I communicate with human spirits, not monsters from some hell dimension. But hey, knock yourselves out!"

As the depleted team walked back along the dim-lit corridors towards Blaisdell's temple, Frankie filmed Denny firing questions at Gould.

"Okay, let's accept your theory of the Interlopers," she said. "But why do they only turn up sometimes? Like, when a crazy, old lord tried devil worship? Or in 1919, when those guys were killed? Why then, but not the hundreds of other years that people lived here?"

"Some people have an affinity for them," said Gould. "Quite unintentionally, some people trigger the PD gateways just by their proximity. Perhaps in ancient times such people were shamans, witches. They could call up the Interlopers, bargain with them."

"Bargain for what?" Denny shot back.

Here, Gould looked uncertain.

"Perhaps persuade them to kill enemies—they would make ideal assassins, able to shape themselves into seductive or terrifying forms. Also, there are numerous legends about good or bad fortune following people who have dealings with supernatural beings. The familiar deal with the Devil is just one variant of a very old idea. These beings may have powers over luck, fate, destiny—there's still so much we don't know. But we're keen on finding out."

"But what do they want?" she persisted. "Why do they kidnap people, kill people? Or try to replace them?"

"What are we doing here?" Gould riposted. "Research, experiment."

"You mean they're scientists, too?" asked Matt.

"I think they're trying to understand us better," replied Gould. "And I don't think they're doing their research out of a love of abstract knowledge. I think they have a higher purpose. A goal in mind."

"Bet it doesn't end in hugs and puppies," commented Frankie, sourly.

They arrived at the temple doorway. The interior was pitch black. Gould took a handful of small flares from his backpack. He explained, as they worked by chemical reaction, they should not be affected by any fluctuations in electrical power. He lit the first flare then threw the small metal tube onto the floor at the bottom of the staircase.

"Okay, who goes first?" asked Matt, standing at the back of the group.

"Not you, apparently," Denny replied, and stepped inside. Gould's flare emitted a bright pinkish glow that made the circular chamber look even more unworldly. The murals, in the flickering light, almost seemed alive. She clicked on her flashlight and picked her way carefully down the stairs, keeping her attention focused on the mass of stone in the center of the room. Behind her Frankie followed, filming the screen while keeping Denny's head and shoulders just in shot.

"I got that screech in my cans again, like feedback only worse," Frankie said, lifting her headphones with a grimace. "Could be a sign of something wicked coming this way."

Denny reached the cellar floor and paused for a moment, taking in the scene. So far as she could tell, nothing had changed. She swept the flashlight beam across the floor, picked out their own footprints in the dust. Then she paused, swung the light back to the altar. Shadows danced, but so far as she could see, they were all cast by her light.

"Heads up," warned Frankie, "I'm getting visual interference now. Snow on the screen."

At the same moment, Denny's flashlight began to flicker then faded to a dull orange glow. Gould struck another flare, threw it over by the altar past Denny.

"Hey you guys, I need help!"

Everyone turned to look up at the top of the stairs. Denny could just make out a stocky figure staring down at them.

"Jim!" she shouted. "Did something happen?"

"It's Brie," came the reply. "Hurry!"

Frankie swung around and pointed her camera up at the doorway just in time to see Jim look to one side then run off along the corridor out of sight.

"What's wrong with Brie?" Denny called, dashing up the stairs. "Jim?"

She heard Gould shouting something but could not make out the words. She rounded the corner, hesitated. A figure was standing about ten yards away, just outside the feeble glow of the light in the corridor.

"Jim?" she said, suddenly doubtful.

The being that had mimicked Jim crouched, its pale limbs elongating, and bounded towards Denny. She saw small, black eyes, a face that was flowing even as the creature hurled itself forward. It snarled, held up claws that now only bore a vague resemblance to human hands. Denny screamed and ran back into the cellar. In her panic, she stumbled halfway down the stairs, fell, and landed hard. Piercing pain shot through her right ankle.

"Jesus Christ," exclaimed Matt, who was halfway up the stone stairway. "What is it?"

"One of them!" shouted Gould. "Get it on film!"

"Still running," Frankie said, aiming her camera up at the doorway. "Poor quality, better than nothing."

They waited for the Interloper to appear in the doorway, but the portal remained empty. Denny glanced round, seeing puzzlement vying with anxiety on her colleagues' faces. Then she saw something else. The air behind Frankie was starting to shimmer. Denny remembered Gould's description, and opened her mouth to shout a warning. Before she could make a sound, however, a pale, elongated figure materialized. The Interloper wrapped long, thin arms around Frankie, who yelled out in alarm and let go of her camera. Denny was struggling to stand when the first creature appeared, bounding down the stairs. It shot past Gould and Matt before the men could respond and joined its companion. Between them they easily lifted the struggling Frankie off her feet.

"Help her!"

Gould and Matt were both frozen with shock, and by the time Denny had staggered upright, Frankie had been dragged into the shimmering sphere. The abduction had taken seconds. Denny fell to her knees, starting to weep with anger and confusion.

"It was her all along," said Gould, in a stunned voice. "They sensed her. I thought it was one of the psychics, but it was her."

"What are you talking about?" shouted Denny. "We need to do something!"

"You gonna go into that thing?" demanded Matt, pointing at the sphere of turbulent air as he backed towards the stairs. "Because I'm outta here!"

"Sure, run away!" Denny cried. "That's your specialty!"

She stood again, sobbing at the pain, and started to limp forward. Gould grabbed her arm, refused to be shaken off. She began to beat at him with her free hand.

"You can't," he said firmly. "Believe me, it's pointless. It's been tried. If you knew what—"

Gould stopped, staring past Denny, who turned to look into the weird gateway to an unimaginable reality. The shimmering globe was darker, pulsing, growing. It turned almost opaque, and then a hand appeared, clawing at the air. Denny stopped struggling, fell back against Gould.

"Don't just stand there, you assholes!" Matt shouted from the doorway. "They're coming for us all!"

"No!" Denny shouted, hoping against hope. "It's Frankie, she's trying to get back!"

She staggered forward and made a grab for the hand, only realizing as she grasped the fingers that it was way too large to be Frankie's. She tried to pull free but now she was gripped tight. A vague bulk was materializing in the air in front of her, forming three feet above the floor.

"Get away!" Denny shouted, breaking free with a tremendous effort. She fell backwards just as the stranger emerged fully from the weird portal and collapsed onto the cellar floor. A wave of the now-familiar stench washed over Denny then the shimmering globe vanished.

"What is it?" Matt yelled.

Good question, thought Denny, as she pushed herself on her behind away from the grotesque figure that had appeared. *Is this a human or not?*

At first, she thought the figure might be an Interloper taking the form of a Halloween scarecrow. But then she saw the tell-tale marks of old wounds on the head and hands, and a few strands of gray hair on the head. Denny decided that she was looking at a tall, painfully thin man clad in ragged clothes that—she realized—must once have been expensive finery. The newcomer wore a long coat, now mostly black with dirt, but she glimpsed of a lining of red silk. A single, tarnished, silver button still clung to the coat, which had lost most of one sleeve.

But the man's face was far more ravaged than his garments. It was much-lined, deathly white, with dark staring eyes that showed white all around. Denny's flashlight, dropped in the confusion, suddenly flared brightly, restored to full power. At the sudden illumination, the stranger gave a choking cry and covered his face with his hands. His fingernails were long and ragged, but again they looked distinctly human. Then the stranger croaked out a single word.

"Light!"

"Is it one of them?" Matt asked, his voice revealing uncertainty. "It doesn't look too dangerous."

No, he's not nearly agile enough, thought Denny, as the stranger huddled on the floor, quivering. *This looks like a regular human.*

"Who are you?" she managed to ask, trying to sound nonthreatening.

The stranger uncovered his face, gazed at her open-mouthed.

"Who," he said, as if sounding out the simple English word. "Who?"

The ravaged face contorted in bafflement, as if Denny had posed an immensely difficult problem. Gould stepped forward, bent over the prone figure.

"Is it George?" Gould asked, in a coaxing tone, as if speaking to a small child. "George, yes?"

The ragged man uncovered his face, gazed up at Gould.

"George?" he gasped, then gave a crazy grin. "Yes. Yes!"

"Ladies and gentlemen," he said. "I think this is our host. Lord George Blaisdell."

"Aw, you're crazy!" scoffed Matt, who had paused halfway up the stairway. "That guy vanished, what, two hundred years ago. Right? How could he be here now?"

"George," the stranger repeated. "Lord, yes. Was a lord."

The newcomer accepted Gould's offer of a hand and got slowly to his feet. Denny stepped forward and took the man's other arm, helped lead him to the steps, where he sat down. As she helped George hobble slowly across the chamber, she saw that the back of his coat had been torn open lengthwise, as had the garments underneath.

"Gould," she said. "There's something on his back."

The object sticking between Blaisdell's shoulders was like a huge cyst. A little larger than a baseball, it was dull brown and pulsed like a beating heart. From it radiated black strands that vanished under the man's skin.

"Don't touch it!" Gould warned. "It might be dangerous!"

"I wasn't going to touch it," replied Denny. "I'm not crazy! But what the hell is it?"

The growth on the man's back looked something like a fungus, but its pulsation reminded her of documentaries about weird deep-sea creatures.

Could it be some kind of disease, she wondered. *Or a parasite from the Phantom Dimension?*

Gould began to fire questions at the man, repeatedly calling him George, trying to establish his identity for certain. But the stranger just stared, open-mouthed, at Gould. Denny raised her hand for silence and drew on her own journalistic experience.

Okay, never ask a question with a simple Yes or No answer. Always get the person to tell their story.

"George," she said gently, "where have you been?"

The thin, shabby man looked up at her, and for a moment Denny feared that he might be too far gone to tell them anything. She thought of traumatized veterans, accident victims, and the abused and damaged who struggled to face their pasts. But then the stranger put his hands to the sides of his head and screamed.

"Hell! I have been in Hell!"

***

Matt ran along the hallway, fuming silently at the idiocy of Denny and Gould, determined to get out of Malpas Abbey as soon as possible.

Screw the goddamn show, he thought. *To hell with them all. Captain Matt's not gonna go down with this ship.*

He reached the main hall and was about to head back toward the kitchen when he stopped, struck by a simple idea. The Mercedes was, according to Jim, still at the gates. The keys would be in the ignition. Even if they weren't, Matt could hot-wire a car. It was one of many skills he had acquired in his adolescent years.

They'll still have Gould's car, he reasoned. *It's not like I'm actually abandoning them.*

Smiling to himself, he went to the front door and opened it. As the chill night air blew in a spray of rain, he hesitated.

What if there are more of those things outside?

Matt looked around, gazed for a moment at the jumbled heap of rotten remains that Jim had dropped onto the hall floor. That Interloper was safely dead, and he had seen two others drag Frankie through the gateway. He hefted his flashlight. The large, rubber-encased torch made a decent club.

How many of the sneaky little bastards can there be? Maybe they're all gone now.

Rather than dwell on possible answers, Matt set off into the night, slamming the door behind him. The noise was so loud that he flinched slightly. Anyone nearby would have heard it. Or anything. He set off at a steady jog along the driveway, the flashlight flickering between full power and near-failure. As he got further from the house, though, the light from the torch became steadier.

Gould was right about his weird physics stuff, Matt thought. *A lot of good it will do him if more of those things come through after that George character.*

Now he could see the bulk of the Mercedes ahead, gleaming in the rain. The driver's door was open, and as he climbed in, he saw Jim's keys dangling from the ignition. Slamming the door, he started the engine, flicked on the headlights. The beams illuminated the way to safety. Matt felt himself grow even more tense as he saw how little separated him from freedom and safety.

Put that pedal to the metal, he thought. *And in five seconds, I'm on the road back to the sane world. Back to reality.*

"Were you really going to leave me, baby?"

Denny's face, her eyes huge and dark, appeared in the driving mirror. At the sight of her, Matt felt his all-too-familiar emotions wash over him. There was confusion and guilt at his decision to run out on her, his intense desire to possess her again, but above all, resentment at the way she had ended their relationship.

"Denny?" he said. "How did you—"

"I ran after you," she said simply. "Remember, I was a track star? You always said I had great legs. Among other attributes."

She reached over and ruffled his hair, and he saw that she was naked.

No, he thought, with a sudden stab of fear. *No way is this really her. This is one of them.*

"Get out," he snapped, picking up the heavy flashlight. "Get away from me you freak!"

"Aw, you got me," said the Interloper, leaning forward to put her face a few inches from his. "But I had you fooled for a second, right? You really wanted it to be her. For her to come crawling back to you."

Matt did not bother to reply, but instead brought the torch down on the creature's head. There was a sickening crunch, and the monster emitted a pathetic yelp, and fell backwards.

"Oh, you really hurt me, Matt!" it whined, holding its pale hands over the wound. Dark fluid oozed between its long fingers. "No wonder they always end up leaving you!"

"Shut up," he grunted, trying to land another blow. But this time the Interloper was too quick for him. Sharp-clawed talons grabbed his wrist, and they began to struggle for the flashlight. Matt punched at the creature's face but it dodged, moving with alarming speed. Its limbs seemed to be elongating during the fight, the pale body that had been so like Denny's became distorted, a caricature of humanity. And as it lost its seductive form, it became stronger.

Gotta kill it quick, he thought desperately. *Beat its goddam brains out.*

"Should have played along, baby," the Interloper hissed through its hideous, needle-like teeth. "Now there's gonna be none of the pleasure, just all of the pain."

***

"Calm down, George," Denny said, patting his shoulder. "You're safe now."

"What do you mean, George?" Gould asked. "Why do you say you were in Hell?"

"Because the Devil took me there, you silly girl!" replied George, his British accent now very obvious. "I taunted him, took his name in vain, and he came for me. He killed the others, I saw him do it—but me, he took. He chose me to torment for all eternity. Or so I thought."

Denny detected a hint of pride in the way George talked of his abduction. The man was pleased, even after his horrendous ordeal, to have been singled out by the Prince of Darkness—as he undoubtedly saw the Interloper that had taken him.

Maybe he is an old-time aristocrat, she thought. *He gives off that kind of vibe. But could someone live for over two hundred years in the Phantom Dimension?*

"What was it like?" Gould demanded, leaning over George. "Is it a world like ours?"

"Like?" said George, quietly. "There are black stars in a pale sky, living stars that watch you. The sky hurts your eyes, the stars mock you! Cruel stars, hungry stars! And there are things like trees, but with eyes, and mouths, and they walk on their roots. The demons that took me can change their shape, strange beasts. Some squirm, some burrow! They took me into their vile catacombs to be tortured, humiliated, starved. But everywhere is in a great turmoil, a fierce wind blows down from the black stars, sears the skin, scours the mind of reason..."

The monologue trailed off and George stared vacantly. A thin trickle of drool fell from one side of his mouth.

"How long were you there?" Denny asked.

The pale, withered face turned up toward her again.

"No days or nights in Hell," George mumbled. "No way to tell the time. An eternity, a moment, who can tell?"

"A night under the hill," murmured Gould, eyes wide. "That fits."

Denny frowned at her colleague, but before she could ask him what he meant, he went on, "We have to get this man some medical help."

Gould helped the stranger to his feet.

"Come on, George," he said, "let's get you to the kitchen, at least it's warm there."

Denny joined Gould and between them they aided the limping, wheezing George up the stairway. At the door, they paused for a moment to look back. There was no sign of the spherical disturbance that marked the gateway to the Phantom Dimension.

"What if it's closed for good?" she asked.

"It always opens again, eventually," Gould replied. "Come on, let's get him to the others. That First-Aid kit will come in handy again."

**

"Did you hear a scream?" asked Jim.

"Maybe," whimpered Brie. "They shouldn't have gone back to that evil place!"

Jim was changing the dressing on Brie's cheek while Marvin paced back and forth in the kitchen. The single light bulb that lit the room faded again, flickered, then returned to full strength.

"Hold still," warned Jim. "I need to swab it with antiseptic. Then I'll put on a fresh dressing."

"Does it look real bad?" asked Brie. "It feels numb. Frozen. What if it's infected with something—something alien, something nobody can cure?"

"It's fine," Jim insisted, finishing up. "Just a nasty scratch. You'll be good as new after a few days."

The hell she will, Marvin thought, looking at Brie's face. *That's a festering wound. If she looks in a mirror, she will lose it big time.*

Even in the weak light, he could see that the injury had turned black and seemed to be spreading via dark filaments under Brie's skin.

"God, you people are idiots," snorted Marvin, resuming his pacing. "We should just leave."

"If you want to help," said Jim, "you could go and get the Mercedes. The keys are still in the ignition. I might even have left the engine running. Take my flashlight."

Now you're taunting me, Marvin thought. *Calling me a coward. They're always mocking me, trivializing my contribution.*

"Maybe I will," he replied, pleased at the surprised expression on Jim's face. "Way you tell it, these things play on fear. Well, I'm a grown-up, so no boogeyman's going to scare me."

Jim's face now showed concern, and some irritation.

"It would be stupid to go alone," he said, standing up. "I'll go with you."

Marvin felt relieved, but Jim's offer prompted Brie to have a full-on panic attack. Jim had to sit back down and speak soothingly to her to stop her hyperventilating. As Brie would not come outside with them, the Englishman concluded that they had no choice but to stay with her.

"Nah, I'll go anyway," Marvin said, trying to sound casual. "End of the driveway, right?"

"At least take a weapon of some kind," Jim said, looking around the kitchen. "There must be something you could use."

Marvin glanced around the stark kitchen, then picked up a small saucepan, hefted it. He felt slightly ridiculous, but it was a kind of metal club. He gave what he hoped was a jauntily ironic salute to the others and left. When he reached the hallway and saw the heap of foul remains where Jim had dropped them, he hesitated. The creatures were unearthly, disturbing. But the Interloper had nonetheless been killed in a fight with Jim.

A smack in the head with a cheap saucepan might just be enough, he reasoned. *I'll show them who's the real man of action here. Cool, decisive. Gets the job done.*

As he stepped outside and slammed the door behind him, Marvin was already visualizing his success. He would walk back into the kitchen, throw the dented pan into the sink, then casually remark that everyone's ride was ready.

With his free hand, he flicked on the flashlight, played the beam around the area just outside the house. There was nothing to see but gravel, weeds, mud. A gust of wind blew a spray of rain into his face

Nothing to be scared of, he thought. *These Interlopers are just glorified vermin, when you think about it. Stand up to them and they'll run, or get their heads smashed in.*

Marvin set off down the driveway. He began to whistle a jaunty tune, then thought better of it and stopped.

CHAPTER 7

NIGHT MOVES

"Who the hell is this?" demanded Jim, jumping up from the table.

"Good question," Denny replied, as she and Gould helped George to a chair.

By now, the stranger had recovered some composure and was staring around him with obvious curiosity. He still seemed confused and afraid, though. George allowed himself to be seated, leaning forward so that the bizarre growth on his back did not touch the back of the chair.

"Jim, I think this is Lord George Blaisdell himself," Gould began. "But before we talk about that, let's try and help him. Perhaps some water?"

Jim offered George a plastic bottle of spring water. The stranger stared at the container, took it gingerly, then poured a little of its contents onto his hand. Then George drank, sipping cautiously at first before greedily gulping down the entire bottle. Brie, who had been gazing in puzzlement at the newcomer, got up and offered him a candy bar. Again he seemed puzzled, and Brie had to show him how to unwrap it, and then mime taking a bite.

If he's never seen a Snickers, Denny thought, *maybe he is from a bygone age.*

"What about that parasite, or whatever it is?" she asked Gould. "Will it die eventually, in our world?"

Gould looked startled at her suggestion, then frowned.

"You know, that's a very sensible notion, based on what we know," he said, drawing her aside and speaking in a low voice. "I'm impressed by how cool you are about all this. But if that strange organism is somehow part of his circulatory system, its death—for whatever reason—could harm him. Trying to remove it would be very risky, of course."

Gould glanced over to where Jim and Brie were tentatively speaking to George, who was not making much sense.

"To be honest, I've no idea how to proceed. This seems to combine the paranormal with the medical in a grim way."

"Guess doctors at a regular hospital would be as baffled as we are," Denny mused. "But we can't just leave him here. We've got to take him to safety!"

Gould nodded.

"The foundation has its own medical division," he said. "I'll call them in. It's time they sent help anyway. Things have gone much farther than I imagined."

"That's quite the understatement," murmured Denny.

While Gould stepped outside to use his phone, Denny brought the others up to speed on what had happened. Brie and Jim were both stunned to learn that Frankie had simply vanished. Denny, for her part, was amazed to learn that Marvin had gone alone to help the group.

"And Gould thinks this bloke is Blaisdell?" Jim said, staring at George, who was now sitting with a vacant expression, chin smeared with chocolate. "Really? We're talking about time travel?"

"Gould said something about a 'night under the hill'," Denny recalled. "Does that mean anything?"

"Fairies," said Brie, surprising Denny. "In the old days they said a night under the hill with the Little People was a kind of time-twisting event. A man who went away with them would return, not having aged. But he'd find his family all dead and gone, his home in ruins, and himself a forgotten man. Time just flows differently there."

Jim was shaking his head as Brie put her theory across.

"That thing we saw was nothing like Tinkerbell," he pointed out. "If we're looking for fantasy creatures, the Interlopers are like demons. Or Morlocks."

"No, I get that," Brie said, becoming more animated. "But the Victorians prettified the way we see all our folklore! The term 'Fairie' once meant another world, a weird, scary place where our laws don't apply. It was only applied to cute little people with wings much later."

"Some medieval scholars called them 'longaevi'," Gould put in. "It means 'the long-lived ones'. As Brie says, they were not originally seen as sweet-natured, but capricious and often destructive. Creatures to placate or avoid, for whom time works differently."

Denny thought about the idea. If Gould and Brie were right, then over two centuries could pass in the human world, while much less than a human lifespan could pass in the Phantom Dimension. She tried to recall how old Blaisdell had been when he had vanished, but could only summon the vague idea that he had been middle-aged.

"George," she said, leaning over the stranger, "can you tell me how old you are?"

The man gawped up at her, then gave a mirthless laugh.

"My dear young lady," he said, again with a touch of aristocratic superiority, "I have not had occasion to celebrate my birthday for some time."

Denny had to smile at that.

You may have been a reprobate, she thought, *but you've got guts— they obviously didn't break you.*

"You're thinking that Frankie has really only been over there for a few seconds?" Jim asked. "Weird notion. But if it's true—"

Denny nodded.

"It means she might not have moved far from the gateway on the other side. Or been moved. If someone went through, they could grab her back. They wouldn't be expecting that."

Realization dawned on Jim's face. He shook his head emphatically.

"Oh, come on," he protested, "you're not proposing that I actually go and look for her!"

Denny felt a surge of anger. Jim had fallen short of her expectations.

"No, I want to go," she retorted. "But I need somebody with your background on my side. Think of it as rescuing a hostage from enemy territory,

Jim still looked doubtful.

"Okay, suppose you throw yourself through that—that hole in the air. How could you be sure you'll find your way back?"

"I could be secured with a tow rope," said Denny. "You must have one in your car, or Gould's?"

"Well, yeah, there is one," Jim began, clearly not convinced. "But it seems a bit crude as a way of exploration in another dimension."

"Needs must," she replied. "Better a crude way than do nothing at all."

Denny turned to George again.

"How did you escape?" she asked. "What did you do?"

George's eyes seemed to lose focus as he struggled to recall. His forehead corrugated in a frown.

"I—I can't remember clearly," he said. "I was in their cursed burrow one minute, the next I was falling back into God's true creation."

"Did they let you go?" Denny asked.

"Let him go?" put in Jim, incredulous. "Why would they?"

"No, no, she may be right!" exclaimed George. "I was a captive, then I was free. All else is a blur of pain and confusion. I simply remember the black globe, I knew it offered escape..."

As George trailed off again, Jim stood up and stepped back from the table.

"That sounds fishy. Maybe he's not human, now," he said. "Maybe they've changed him."

Brie, alarmed, got up to cling to Jim, eyes wide with fear.

"No need to get paranoid, guys," said Denny, moving closer to George and gripping the ragged shoulder of the man's coat. "Whatever they did to him, he's still a human being. One of us. We can't turn against each other. That's probably what they want. They seem to thrive on negative emotions in some way."

Jim seemed set to argue, but was interrupted when Gould re-entered the kitchen from the old walled garden. He was damp from the rain, and looked frustrated.

"I can't get a signal," he said. "Maybe one of you could—"

Then Gould paused, puzzled, and looked around the kitchen.

"Hang on—where's Matt?" he asked. "Didn't he come back here?"

"Maybe he met up with Marvin," Jim suggested.

"Shouldn't they both be back by now?" Denny asked.

***

The keys were still in the Mercedes, though the engine had stopped. Feeling pleased with himself, Marvin got into the vehicle and slammed both front doors. He was quickly aware of the foul stench that had come from the corpse of the Interloper.

"Guess I can live with that," he said, starting the engine, then twisting around to reverse up the driveway. But then he eased his foot off the gas and smiled to himself.

I could just drive into that city, whatever it's called, and get a bed for the night. Why take risks? I owe them nothing.

The thought tempted him for a couple of moments, but then he rejected it.

"I may be a selfish asshole," he said firmly, "but I am not a monster."

Besides, he thought, *I can't abandon him—*

Marvin suppressed the thought, squirming in discomfort. He revved the engine and then commenced reversing the big SUV, squinting into the darkness. He had to move very slowly, and toyed with the notion of turning around, but was not prepared to risk going off the track. He was concentrating so hard that the knock on a side window took him by surprise. In the gloom, peering through the rain-spattered glass, he could just make out Matt's leather jacket.

"Jesus Christ!" he shouted, stopping the car. "Matt, what the hell are you doing?"

"Sorry!" came the reply, as Matt lugged the door open and climbed inside.

"What's going on?" demanded Marvin. "I thought you were filming in the cellar?"

"That's finished," the other man replied, staring out of the windshield. "Hey, I got an idea. Let's just go."

Marvin stared for a moment, wondering if he really had heard Matt suggest they ditch the others. Matt's face, smiling brightly now, turned to face him.

"Yeah, I mean it, Marv. Just you and me, let's blow this joint. There are too many of those freak things around. I killed one just now, threw its corpse into the bushes. So, what do you say, big fella?"

Marvin felt a hand on his knee, and looked down to see slender, pale fingers kneading his plump thigh.

Oh God, no, this is too much.

"Matt," he said, trying to sound composed. "This is hardly the time—"

"Aw come on, big guy," said Matt, his tone playful. "We both know it. I could see how broken up you were when I was with Denny, that little surge of hope when we broke up."

Matt's almost too-handsome face leaned closer in the dim light.

"I saw it all. I know just how you feel."

Can't be happening, Marvin thought. *But it is, oh God, I never believed—*

"You never believed I could fall for a selfish old queen with a hairpiece and a big ol' belly like yours?" asked Matt, his tone more teasing now. "Oh, ye of little faith."

"What? Marvin exclaimed. "I don't understand. You said—"

He stopped, feeling a terrible chill run through him. He could see the collar of Matt's pale blue shirt, now, and it was stained with an irregular patch of black. The face that was looking into his was, he realized, a brilliant facsimile of Matt's. But it was a little too good-looking, devoid of any blemish or line. A kind of mask.

"Yeah," said the Interloper, "actually Matt always thought you were a big joke. Guess the joke's on him now, though, huh? What's left of him."

Oh, shit, shit, shit!

Marvin began to fumble at the fastening of his seatbelt. Matt's hand suddenly gripped his flesh so hard that Marvin cried out in pain. The belt came free and he tried to open the driver's door, but the creature was fast and way too strong. It pinned him against his seat and straddled him. It gripped his face in long, inhumanly strong fingers.

"You don't want to run away with me after all!" wailed the Interloper. "Is that any way to treat a regular guy? Maybe I can change your mind."

"Let me go!" Marvin screamed, all self-control gone. "I've done nothing wrong, I don't deserve this!"

"Oh, Marvin," said the creature, shaking its head. "That's not how it works. You make us what we are. Don't you get that?"

It leaned closer, and he saw that what had been a well-defined mouth and chin had bulged out into a weird snout. The being nuzzled at this neck as he whimpered in terror.

"You make us what we are," it repeated. "We are the captives of your wildest hopes, your darkest fears. And if you're kind of pretentious, so are we!"

"Leave me alone!" Marvin yelled, struggling in vain to free himself from the Interloper's grip.

"Can't do that," replied the entity. "There's only two ways this can end. You get away and reveal a bit too much, or you don't. And as we've already got ourselves a fine, young specimen..."

Marvin felt sharp teeth bite into the side of his neck. A gush of warmth spread over his shoulder. With a tremendous effort, he shoved the creature away, and roared with pain as the Interloper tore away a chunk of his flesh while falling backwards. Marvin opened the car door and, clutching at his wound, fell out onto the driveway.

"Don't leave me, Marv! We've got a good thing going here!"

Even in his abject terror, Marvin still recognized lines from the fantasies he had rehearsed so often in his mind. The monster that was not Matt was, he dimly realized, picking ideas and phrases from his mind.

They're emotional vampires, he thought, staggering upright and starting to stumble towards Malpas Abbey. *They feed on our emotions.*

"Close, but no cigar!" the creature snarled, as it landed on his shoulders and bore him to the ground. "We don't feed on your feelings, we suffer from them. That's why we have to end you. All of you."

Even if Marvin had had the presence of mind to ask what that meant, he was soon unable to say anything at all.

*****

"Nobody's got a signal?" asked Gould.

Jim, Denny, and Brie all shook their heads. George looked on, clearly baffled as to why four people were staring forlornly at small, glowing rectangles.

"Could be the signal drops off at night," Gould went on. "Maybe if we were nearer to the village."

"What village?" Denny asked.

"You dozed off," Brie explained. "We passed through one on the way."

"Malpas Village is just a dozen houses and a church," Jim explained. "I noticed a cell mast on the church tower. It's about half a mile away."

"Okay," said Brie, with a touch of her normal perkiness, "let's all go there! Go to the village, get help."

"No!" Denny found herself standing between the others and the door, holding up a hand. "We don't leave anyone behind if we can help it. Jim, I need that rope."

A predictable argument ensued, with Brie insisting on leaving and

Jim tending to agree with her. Gould seemed undecided, almost furtive. But they all fell silent when George stood up and walked over to Denny.

"You are more courageous than the men here, lass," he said. "Has manliness fallen out of favor in England? I see women wear breeches, now."

Jim guffawed out loud, but Denny felt oddly moved.

"At least he gets it!" she shouted. "Are we going to try and help Frankie or just run away?"

"I'll help," said Gould simply.

"We'll give it a go, and we'll all stick together," added Jim. "Nobody goes off alone."

***

In the village pub, two men drinking at a corner table received simultaneous text messages.

"Benson?" said the older man, looking at his phone.

The younger man nodded.

"Looks like Gould hasn't reported in on schedule."

The two rose and, leaving their pints unfinished, went out into the rainy night. Behind them, a handful of locals watched them leave without staring, then began talking about the Abbey, and what might be going on there.

The two men got into an unmarked white van, then the older man took out his phone again. He held it midway between them before making the call.

"Control, what's up?"

"What is up," came Benson's voice, "is that Gould has been out of touch for over two hours. You and Davenport get up there and reconnoiter. Do not intervene, merely check the lie of the land."

"What if they're in trouble?" said Davenport.

"Report that they're in trouble and try to establish the nature of said trouble and how much there is of it," Benson's voice responded.

"That is all."

The call ended. The two agents exchanged a look.

"He's a cold-blooded bastard," said Davenport. "Like a reptile in a two thousand quid suit."

"And he's the boss," replied Forster, starting the engine. "Never forget that."

They did not speak again until they reached the turn-off to Malpas Abbey. As the van climbed the shallow gradient towards the estate, a light mist appeared. It gradually grew denser until it was thick enough to cut visibility to about ten yards.

"Foggy all of a sudden," remarked Davenport.

"We're in the countryside in autumn," said Forster. "Not exactly surprising."

"Doesn't mist tend to lie in the valleys? We're going uphill," the younger man pointed out.

"Here we are," said Forster.

The van's headlights showed the stone pillars marking the main gates. The fog inside the gateway was so dense that it formed a silver-gray wall.

"We can always get out and walk up to the house," Davenport said slowly. "Though of course we might just fall into an ornamental pond in this muck."

Forster grunted noncommittally, then took out his phone. He tried to call Benson, and failed.

"This is not normal," insisted Davenport. "We should go back."

"No," said Forster, firmly. "I'm in charge. We can't ask for new orders, so I say we go in. Get the gear out."

"Can't we at least drive up the doorway?" whined Davenport.

"Oh yeah," said the older man, sarcastically. "Why not hire a brass band to march along behind us, just so everyone knows we're coming? Stealth recon, you nitwit."

The two men climbed out into the damp night air, walked around the van, and opened the rear doors. Forster took out a double-barreled shotgun, handed it to Davenport, then picked up an identical weapon. Davenport frowned at the gun.

"You'd think the boss could run to something more effective than this," he grumbled. "The world's awash with assault rifles, and we're equipped to shoot bloody pheasants."

"Benson draws the line at illegal handguns, apparently," said Forster. "Here, take a taser and a baton. You never know."

Forster got himself a First-Aid kit and two sets of night vision goggles.

"Right," he said. "Now we're suitably equipped, let's go and visit one of the stately homes of England."

***

"Here's how we do this," said Denny. "We stick together, look after our wounded, get them to the vehicle. Then Jim drives them into Chester for medical treatment, right?"

Jim and Gould exchanged a glance, then nodded.

"Seems like the right thing," Jim said.

"Ted," Denny went on, "will you stay and be my backup?"

Gould hesitated.

"If I stay, there has to be some kind of time limit," he said finally. "I can't just wait for you to come back. Can it be half an hour?"

"Make it at least an hour," Denny insisted. "Because that won't be very long on the other side. Just a few minutes, in fact."

"True," Gould conceded.

Jim and Gould armed themselves with kitchen knives, while Denny selected a glass rolling pin. Then the three of them ushered Brie and George out to the hallway. The group skirted the Interloper's remains, but George hung back to peer more closely at the mess of rotted tissue and pale bones.

"A dead demon!" he exclaimed. "I never saw a dead one before. Surely such things are invulnerable by divine ordnance?"

"They're not demons," said Gould. "They're as mortal as you or I."

George looked puzzled at that, and fell silent as they left the hall. They were confronted by a wall of fog. Taken aback, they paused, then Gould and Jim switched on flashlights that shone dimly and flickered.

"When did that roll in?" asked Brie.

"It was clear enough outside a few minutes ago," Gould said. "So..."

"It might not be natural," Denny finished. "Big deal. Let's get to your car, Ted."

Gould's Ford sedan had just come into view when Brie shrieked and fell. In the weak torchlight, Denny saw the woman scrabbling to get up in what looked like a mud puddle. Then she noticed the dark red stains on Brie's hands, the black patches on her denims. Gould's flashlight picked out a heap of wet, sausage-like objects around Brie's feet. Then the flickering radiance fell onto a pale body. The face was distorted in pain, but still recognizable.

"Matt!" Brie screamed, hurling herself away from the horrific scene and colliding with Denny.

Matt's entrails had been torn out and flung across the pathway. His undershorts were still on the body but his shirt, jacket and pants were gone.

It took his clothes, Denny thought, numb with horror, and trying to fight down her rising gorge. *Like they did with Lucy Gould, to make a more convincing fake.*

She turned away from the unbearable sight. Denny felt herself start to grow faint with shock, and staggered across to the car.

"You okay?" asked Jim.

She could only shake her head at first, then managed to say, "Give me a minute."

"Sorry, but time's pressing—do you still want to stay behind?" asked Gould.

Denny looked up at his anxious face, and guessed that he was conflicted, hoping to draw courage from her.

"Nobody's going to judge you for leaving," Jim added. "None of us signed up for this."

Matt's dead, she thought. *I can't help him. Frankie might still be alive. I have to believe that.*

"Ted, I'm still willing to try if you'll back me up," she said.

"Right, I'll get the tow rope," said Gould, unlocking the car and then throwing the keys to Jim. "We'll keep two of the flashlights, you take everything else."

While Jim and Brie tried to persuade the confused George to get into the Ford, Gould and Denny got the rope out of the trunk. As an afterthought, Denny tossed her rolling pin and picked up a heavy wrench.

"This still strikes me as bonkers," grumbled Jim. "You've no idea how to open the way through and even if—"

They all stared around them to see a figure had appeared in the fog, back towards the house. It was barely visible, but Denny could see it was dressed in Matt's clothes.

"A demon!" cried George, scrambling into the car and curling up on the back seat.

The Interloper raised its hand in an ironic salute, then turned and vanished. A couple of seconds later, they heard the sound of the house's great front door opening, then slamming shut.

"It's going back!" breathed Denny. "Come on, Ted!"

CHAPTER 8

THE PHANTOM DIMENSION

"Should we have left them?" asked Brie.

"No choice," Jim replied, peering ahead into the fog.

The Ford's headlights seemed to have little impact on the gray murk. Jim nosed ahead in low gear, but still almost collided with the SUV, which suddenly loomed into view. The big Mercedes was blocking the driveway. Rather than get out, Jim nudged it out of the way.

"That'll piss of Gould," he remarked, with forced jollity. "Still, it's a company car."

"Horseless carriages," said George, from the back seat. "An age of wonders. Are they powered by steam?"

"He's perking up," observed Jim, with a wry smile at Brie. "Want to give him a lecture on internal combustion engines? Maybe move to aviation, the internet?"

Brie managed a weak smile at that, and they set off again.

"Soon, we'll be at the gates," said Jim confidently. "Then it's a clear road to Chester, a nice clean hospital, and for me, a hotel, and a hot shower."

But as they progressed slowly down the fog-bound driveway, the familiar gateposts failed to appear.

"Could we be on the wrong road somehow?" asked Brie, tentatively.

Jim shook his head.

"The house had only one driveway, and we are still on it. If we'd somehow passed the gates without seeing them, we'd be on tarmac, not gravel, so I can only assume—"

Suddenly Jim hit the brakes, and the Ford slewed to one side.

"What the hell?"

"Oh my God," cried Brie.

The SUV was in front of them again, its bulky shape unmistakable despite the fog.

"How did we come around in a circle?" Brie asked.

Jim looked at her, then back at the Mercedes he had shoved out of the way three minutes earlier.

"I'm sure we did not circle round," he said in a monotone. "We were going in a straight line, I'd swear it on a stack of Bibles."

From the back seat, George spoke quietly.

"They will not let us go unless their purpose is served."

***

"Sorry," said Gould breathlessly, catching up with Denny at the entrance to the temple. "I've never been very athletic."

"All the more reason for me to go through while you hold the fort," she replied. "Let's see if our little friend has gone through."

There was no sign of the Interloper in the cellar. But their flashlight revealed the now familiar shimmering sphere in the air, just to the side of the altar. Gould lit another couple of caving flares and threw them down. Then they descended and started their simple preparations.

"Okay," said Denny, "I'm going straight through. You give me an hour, right? Then pull my string, see what happens."

After fastening the rope around her waist, Denny climbed onto the altar and prepared to pitch herself through the gateway. After a moment's thought, she threw her flashlight and the wrench into the portal first. They vanished.

"What if it's a hundred-foot drop on the other side?" asked Gould.

"Then get ready to haul me up, big guy," she replied, and executed a swan dive into what looked like an empty space.

Gould braced himself but the rope did not run out at speed, as he had feared. Instead, it gradually played through his hands in spurts, a few inches at a time, then stopping for several minutes. He checked his watch every few minutes, wondering what would happen if he pulled on the rope and it snapped. Or if, instead of Denny, what came through was an inhuman monster.

Don't imagine the worst, he told himself. *That might make it more likely, given the way these things operate.*

"Fear is the mind killer," he said aloud, then wondered where he had dredged up the quotation. He began to obsess over trivia, trying to remember the names of the current England cricket squad, filling his mind with irrelevant data to suppress any memories or feelings the Interlopers might exploit.

Does Denny have no deep, dark fears? he wondered. *Is that why all she saw was a mishmash of commonplace childish fears?*

An hour had passed, and he gave a gentle pull on the rope. It yielded an inch or two. He wondered if this meant Denny was standing up, or if he was pulling at her inert—maybe dead—body. Gould gave another tug on the rope and felt it give, then become slack. Anxiety mounted as he began to reel it in, hand over hand, wondering whether the slight resistance he felt was from Denny or the strange portal itself.

The question was settled when the end of the towrope appeared and fell to the floor.

"Oh Jesus. What do I do now?"

As in reply, the gateway darkened, swelled, pulsed with strange energy. Gould took a step back as something came through. It was not Denny or an Interloper, but a compact, boxy object. Frankie's camera fell to the floor with a crash, fragments of plastic and glass scattering over the stone slabs.

***

Denny rolled when she landed but the impact still winded her. She felt a stab of pain in her thigh as she landed on something hard. *Flashlight or wrench,* she thought. *Either way I'll have quite a bruise.*

She lay curled up and opened her eyes tentatively. At first, she could see nothing but a swirl of garish colors, the buffeting of a strong wind that was burning hot. She remembered standing in front of a huge industrial oven on an assignment. She squeezed her eyelids shut again, took a tentative breath of the scorching air. There was a smell of burning vying with faint tang of decay in the air, something like a match struck in a moldy bathroom

Opening her eyes again, she looked down and saw that she had fallen onto an uneven surface. It felt rubbery, and looked like dimpled reddish clay. By one of her hands, a pale creature like a centipede writhed then made a dart for her fingers. Denny quickly pulled her hand away, scrambled upright. She picked up her flashlight and wrench, holding the latter ready as a club. But nothing else appeared to threaten her.

At least I can breathe the air, she thought. *I'd look pretty dumb if I was poisoned or suffocated in the first ten seconds.*

In front of Denny, the reddish ground extended away in all directions. It seemed utterly featureless as first. But as her eyes adjusted to the peculiar light, Denny saw that she was at the top of a shallow rise. Ahead of her was a bleak plain, dotted by black blotches that might have been clumps of trees. There were also some more regular shapes, straight lines that might have been walls. It was hard to get a sense of size or distance, however. The light was dim yet also oddly painful, a purplish radiance that made her think of ultraviolet.

Denny looked behind her at the gateway. Instead of a rippling sphere of disturbed air, the gateway on this side was a pitch-black globe, roughly a yard across. It hovered about four feet above the ground. Beneath the sphere, she saw smoke rising from an area of blackened soil, yet she felt no radiant heat on her face and hands. Unable to make sense of the phenomenon, she filed the observation away for future reference. Then she looked up.

"Oh my God!"

The sky was a shimmering, silvery color. There were a few ragged shreds of reddish cloud. There was no sun or moon, just a general luminosity streaming down onto the wasteland below. Above the clouds were the black stars George had ranted about. They were star-like in that they twinkled, throwing out flashes of green and orange light. But there the resemblance ended. These stars were, she felt sure, living creatures of some sort. They moved relative to one another. They looked like huge black starfish, their arms waving lazily. But at the center of each black star was a gleaming disk.

Eyes. They have eyes, just like George said. These stars really do look down.

Shuddering, she turned her attention back to the landscape of the Phantom Dimension. There was no sign of any thing living other than dozens of the centipede-like bugs. Then she saw something out of place nearby, a dark object with straight edges. It seemed familiar, even in the deceptive light. Denny walked toward it, feeling her feet sink into the ground, hearing a squelching over the howling of the wind.

It was Frankie's camera. Already some strange process had half-buried the bulky piece of equipment in the reddish earth. As she squatted to look closer, Denny saw that the ground itself was heaving and sucking at the camera. She looked down at her feet. What she had taken for a kind of dirt was acting like a living thing and throwing eager tendrils up and over her shoes.

If I don't keep moving, I'm dead.

Denny wrenched her feet free of the hungry ground and tried to remember how to work the camera. As she tinkered, she flicked on the built-in light, and a pool of blue-white radiance revealed the dirt to be bright ocher. A pale, sinuous creature writhed in apparent discomfort, then scuttled for the shadows. She followed the worm-like animal with the beam, watching its intense reaction as it tried to escape. Then, feeling slightly guilty, she turned off the light.

Maybe what we think of as normal light is painful to some of the things that live here.

Denny filed the idea away as potentially useful and started to circle the camera, looking for footprints. Then she told herself not to be so dumb, as it was clear that the nature of this alien dirt would have erased any tracks. She raised the viewfinder to the horizon, hoping to see a structure, some sign of intelligence. A tall, tapering shape might have been an obelisk of some kind.

But that's way too far to walk, so long as I'm tethered by this rope.

Denny lowered the camera, focused on details that were maybe a hundred yards away. Now she could see that what she had taken for a wall seemed to be the remains of a collapsed building. As she swung the camera around, more apparent ruins appeared peeking out of the ruddy earth. It occurred to Denny that she was standing in the middle of what had been a settlement of some sort. But it had long since been abandoned.

Why? Something to do with the gateway to our world?

Now a dark blur that resembled a clump of trees came into view. It consisted of dark, thick trunks supporting a canopy of oval, fleshy leaves. Then one 'trunk' lifted itself out of the ground, moved toward her, replanted itself. The supposed clump was walking, coming her way. She recalled that George had said something about trees with eyes. Denny lowered the camera, scanned her surroundings with the naked eye. She wondered if the half dozen or so dark blurs were nearer than when she had arrived.

She focused again on the distant, pylon-like object. She could see now that it was in fact one of many, as other more-or-less conical forms were just visible on the horizon. Denny reasoned that she might be looking at a city, the Interloper equivalent of Manhattan. The things might be the skyscrapers of the Phantom Dimension. But it seemed improbable, given the apparent ruins around her. She felt strongly that this was a world in an advanced stage of decay.

This was a dumb, desperate idea. They were right. But I had to try.

"Frankie!" she yelled. "Where are you?"

Her voice sounded oddly flat, and she could not believe it would carry far. The wind increased to a gale and almost knocked her down.

"Help!"

The voice was almost inaudible over the howling gale. She could not make out the direction it had come from. But it sounded like a woman's voice, high-pitched, desperate.

Did I imagine it?

There was a tremendous yank on the rope, so hard that she fell backwards onto her behind and dropped the camera. Cursing, Denny scrambled to her feet, trying to minimize contact between her skin and the strange, living dirt.

That's already an hour? I've only been here three or four minutes. That's a big-time shift.

Another tug on the rope made her stumble. She hesitated, then heard a faint, plaintive cry. Again, there was no sense of direction, and she looked around, desperately seeking some clue. There were no buildings, but if Frankie could be heard despite the gale she must be nearby. Almost anything seemed possible, including some kind of kind of invisibility cloak.

Underground, Denny thought. *If my world looked like this, I would not live on the surface of it.*

Then she remembered that George had used the word 'burrow'. She pivoted slowly, shielding her eyes, looking for anything that might be an entrance. A dark smear in a low ridge caught her eye. She picked up the camera and zoomed in on it. There was movement in the entrance, a glimpse of what might have been a pallid face. She took a deep breath.

Sorry Ted, she thought. *Only way I can get there is without a safety line.*

She had just dropped the end of the rope to the ground when another jerk pulled it right through the black, pulsating sphere. The only material link to her reality was gone. Denny turned the camera round and looked into the dark lens.

Better make it good. Might be my last words. If anybody ever hears them.

"I'm going underground," she said. "Don't wait for me."

***

"What do you mean?" Jim asked, stopping the car and turning to face George. "Are you saying the Interlopers have got us going around in circles somehow?"

"They are deceivers," George replied, looking from Jim to Brie, as if seeking understanding. "Like all the Devil's minions."

"You mean they created this fog to keep us trapped here?" Brie asked, her voice unsteady. *"They can do that?"*

Great, thought Jim, *she might have a total meltdown if she thinks we can't get away.*

"Just shut up, George," he snapped. "We're safe so long as we're in the vehicle. The worst that can happen is we wait until the fog lifts. Then we'll be able to see the way to the main road."

"But what if it doesn't lift?" demanded Brie, again on the edge of panic.

Jim reached over and took her hand in his.

"I know you've been through a lot," he said. "But think of your son, your husband. You'll see them again if you just—"

Brie, who had been looking out through the windshield, gave a scream and pointed. Looking ahead, Jim could make out two figures emerging from the fog. They were carrying guns, which they pointed at the Ford.

"Crap!" exclaimed Jim, and slammed the car into reverse. Then he paused, staring at the two men as they came closer. "No, hang on, it's all right! I know these guys!"

A couple of minutes later, Forster and Davenport had been brought up to speed on the situation, insofar as Jim could explain things.

"I don't get it," Forster said. "We got in all right, but you can't get out?"

"It's like a force-field, or something," said Davenport. "A one-way portal."

Forster rolled his eyes at Jim.

"The main thing," Forster pointed out, "is that we don't know how many of these Interlopers are still at large, if any. We should go back and check on Gould and the girl, rather than muck around out here."

Brie began to protest at that, but Jim managed to soothe her by pointing out how well-armed the newcomers were.

"These are my old mates from the army," he said. "They're good blokes, they won't let anything happen to you."

"And we've got guns," Davenport added. "Can be useful things, guns."

Jim turned the Ford carefully and they set off back the way they had come. It was only after they had driven a few hundred yards that Jim began to wonder if they could get back to Malpas Abbey, any more than they could reach the main gate.

***

Distances were deceptive. It took Denny far less time than she had expected to reach the burrow, despite the vicious battering from the unceasing wind. She paused at the entrance, which was a roughly circular tunnel about five feet high, sloping sharply downward.

"Hello?" she shouted but heard nothing over the gale. Peering into the dark, she tried to discern movement, but saw nothing other than blackness.

Okay, let's go for it.

She switched on the flashlight, which flickered worryingly and then produced a steady, if weak, beam. Denny began to climb down.

Maybe it was an Interloper, trying to lure me in, she thought. *But why go to so much trouble? Why not just jump me as soon as I arrived?*

Frustration vied with fear as she reflected, once again, about how little she knew about the enemy she was hoping to defy. Creatures that defied natural laws, that could change their appearance, and that drew on people's thoughts and memories. Monsters. How could she defeat a whole world of monsters?

"One at a time," she murmured. "If that's what it takes."

It soon proved impossible to keep upright without using at least one hand for support. Denny shoved the wrench into the waistband of her jeans, reasoning that the flashlight might double as a club.

Also, she thought, *they don't seem to like bright light much. Maybe they're real sensitive to it?*

She continued down until she the tunnel divided. As she hesitated, shining the flashlight into each aperture, she noticed a gleam of metal. Something was half-buried in the dirt floor. When she bent down to examine it, she realized it was the wooden grip of an antique pistol.

"Flintlock. One of George's, maybe?"

She took a moment to examine the area more closely and saw other items from her world. A couple of bottles, a maimed plastic doll, and a badly damaged paperback book all lay around her. She reached down and picked up the book. The covers were missing but a contents page told her it was a collection of stories entitled *The Adventures of Mister Bunnykins.*

"Cute," she said, tossing down the paperback. She noticed then that the mundane debris all seemed to lie at the entrance to the left-hand tunnel. She decided to follow it and discovered more discarded everyday items as she went. As she rounded a corner, she heard a very human-sounding phrase echoing around her.

"Help me!"

This time the sound was clearer, and it was definitely coming from ahead. What's more, the tunnel was leveling off. Ahead of her, the flashlight revealed an opening into a large chamber of some kind.

"Frankie?" she shouted, hoping to hear her name in response. But there was only an inarticulate cry.

Denny entered the cavern, which was about eight feet high and thirty across. Three other tunnels opened into it. There was a figure sprawled against the far wall, legs and arms fastened to the reddish dirt by a network of pale strands. As Denny approached, she could see the fibers were alive, tensing and flexing as the prisoner struggled against their grip. The captive's face and body were almost totally covered by a pale, living web.

"Frankie?"

A moment of intense joy ended when Denny stepped nearer. A few strands of long hair escaped the web-work, while Frankie always cut her hair short. Now Denny could see that the prisoner must be a child, only a shade over four feet tall. A stifled squeal came from the material covering the face.

"Help me, I'm scared!"

It was a little girl's voice, the accent British, the fear in it spurring Denny to frantic action. She shoved her flashlight right up against the white fibers, and they jerked spasmodically in evident discomfort. She dropped the wrench and with her free hand tried to tear the strands away from the head. After a few moments, she had revealed a small, heart-shaped face. The girl gazed up at her, eyes huge with fear.

"Don't be scared, I'm here to help you!" Denny said.

"Are you—are you a real person?" asked the girl.

"Yep," Denny replied, ripping away more of the pale strands to free the girl's right arm. "And we're going to get you home. Help me get this stuff off if you can."

The girl was still for a moment, then began tearing at the living bindings with her small fingers. Soon most of the restraints had been ripped away, though a network of white fibers remained clinging to the girl's body. Beneath the unpleasant web of tissue, she seemed to be wearing badly stained pajamas. The garments were mismatched, the top covered in teddy bears while the pants were pink with green polka dots.

Like they just put her in whatever kids' clothes they could grab when they were in our world, Denny thought.

The webbing gave way and the child fell forward, away from the wall. Denny caught her. Looking down at the thin, fragile body she saw

126

that the pajama top had been ripped open, just like George's shirt. A dark brown nodule, two inches across, clung to the skin between the girl's shoulder blades. Like the one attached to George, it pulsed with alien life.

"Guess that makes both of us human," she murmured. Then she knelt down and put her hands on the girl's shoulders.

"Okay," she said. "I'm Denny, what's your name?"

The girl's blank expression made Denny wonder if she had lost her memory, through trauma or perhaps some stranger process. But then the child seemed to remember.

"My name is Lucy."

***

It had taken Gould a while but he had finally figured out how to work the replay system on the damaged camera. He watched, awe struck, the footage of the transition to the Phantom Dimension during Frankie's abduction. Then he saw Denny appear, shared her reactions to the strange other world, and heard her final message.

Don't wait for me.

Gould felt a sudden pang of guilt. He had allowed someone to venture into the Phantom Dimension with nothing but a can-do attitude. Now he had to decide whether to wait, knowing Denny might never return. He checked the time. It was now just over an hour and a half since Denny had gone through the portal. The longer he left it, the more chance there was of Interlopers coming through and attacking him. He felt a strong desire to cut his losses and run. He sat on the cellar steps, gazing into the shimmering globe.

Am I a coward?

A door slamming in the distance jolted him from his reverie. The sound of voices followed. Gould ran up, back into the house, just in time to encounter Forster and Davenport. The newcomers gave a quick, if slightly garbled, description of the situation outside. Gould updated them on the Denny situation.

"Okay," said Davenport, hefting his gun. "We go through and get her back. In fact, we save both of 'em, right?"

Forster shook his head.

"Not part of the mission, lad," he growled. "And you never go into hostile territory without orders, and then only with preliminary recon. We're staying firmly in this reality."

"Well, give me a bloody weapon and I'll do it!" shouted Gould, angrier with his own indecision than their hesitation.

"Let's not be hasty," soothed Forster. "Why don't we go and see this mysterious gateway of yours?"

***

It took a second to register, then Denny gasped.

"Lucy? Do you have a brother called Edward?"

The child nodded, but before Denny could ask her anything else, there was a screeching sound from one of the other tunnels.

"The monsters are coming back!" hissed Lucy. "They do bad things!"

"You're telling me," Denny replied, taking the girl's hand. "Right, we're gonna run up that tunnel. When we get outside where there's room, I'll carry you. Okay?"

Lucy gazed solemnly up at her new-found friend.

"Okay."

Another screech, louder this time, spurred the two on. Lucy ran stiffly at first but managed to keep up with Denny's brisk pace. As they reached the fork in the tunnels, Denny glanced back and saw several white figures bounding after them.

"Faster!" she urged breathlessly, pushing Lucy ahead of her.

She turned the flashlight back on the Interlopers, but its feeble radiance seemed to have no effect. The pursuers were gaining. Denny hurled the flashlight in frustration and had the satisfaction of seeing it hit one enemy squarely in the face. The Interloper fell squealing into the dirt, but the others were not deterred. By the time the fugitives reached the opening onto the surface, the nearest creature was just ten feet behind.

Denny took out the wrench, preparing to make a last-ditch stand and give Lucy the chance to escape. She gestured towards the black globe, barely visible in the distance.

"Run to that sphere, that's the way out! Go Lucy! Lucy, you gotta run!"

Instead of obeying Denny, the child was standing still. Lucy was looking up at the sky rather than back at their pursuers. The pursuit had stopped, the Interlopers huddled in the entrance to their burrow. And they, too, were looking up.

Denny raised her eyes and saw a vast, black star blotting out much of the sky. The monstrous entity had descended and was now lowering dark, rope-like tendrils towards the two humans. The single, enormous eye swiveled, seemed to focus on Denny. She felt a chill run through her.

"Don't move!" hissed Lucy. "If you move, they see you."

Vague memories of dinosaur movies flashed through Denny's mind.

Predators sense motion, she thought. *Makes sense.*

A black tendril, thick as her thumb, brushed against her shoulder. Denny gave a small scream but remained motionless. The black star was, she now saw, drifting slowly across the sky, gaining height. The prevailing wind was moving it away from them. Already they were out of reach of the trailing tendrils. The Interlopers saw this, too, and began to edge toward the mouth of the tunnel. The movement, albeit slight, seemed to alert the vast, floating entity. The black star stopped drifting, started to descend, its vast eye scanning the ground. But it was moving at a leisurely pace.

"Now or never," said Denny. "When I say run—"

"We run," replied Lucy, smiling for the first time. "Like in 'Doctor

Who'."

CHAPTER 9:
SHOWDOWN

"How long has it been?" asked Brie.

"Eight hours, forty-seven minutes since she went through," said Jim, wearily. "Or about ten minutes since you last asked."

The group had been gathered in the great dining room since the early hours of the morning. They had broken up some old furniture to make a fire. Brie's wound had been dressed again, while George had been given a proper meal and tea, which he gulped down with relish. George had also been found some of Matt's clothes, including a shirt that fitted loosely over the parasite on his back.

Arguments over what to do next had given way to sullen silence, broken by occasional remarks. Between them, the four Romola Foundation men had worked out a rota, with two of them always on watch in the cellar. At the moment, Gould and Forster were on guard at the gateway.

"Is it getting lighter?" Davenport asked. "Hard to tell in this murk."

"What if we never get out?" Brie moaned. "What if we—just starve?"

"No way can this go on forever!" protested Jim. "Whatever those creatures are doing, they've got to run out of energy eventually. Right?"

Jim looked at Davenport for support. The latter nodded, cleared his throat.

"You obviously know the folk tales, Brie," he said. "Beings from the other world can influence space, time, perception—but their powers are strictly limited. They can be killed, they can be outwitted, they can only visit our world for brief spells. All the stories say so."

"But why keep us trapped here at all?" Brie demanded, looking around at the men. "What is it they want?"

George, who was sitting in an armchair nearest the fire, shrugged.

"How can we understand the motives of demons? Tormenting us, that is their delight!"

"You're a ray of sunshine and no mistake," said Davenport sourly.

"It is clearing!" Brie shrieked, jumping up and running to look out the French windows.

The mist, previously a dark gray wall, was definitely growing paler. As they watched, a bright blur in the sky gradually resolved itself into the sun's disc. It was soon so bright they could not look at it directly. In less than a minute, all that remained of the unnatural fog was a ground mist then there was nothing but a crisp, pleasant autumn morning.

"We can get away!" exclaimed Brie, jumping up and actually clapping her hands with joy.

"Okay, everyone outside to the vehicles," said Jim. "I'll go and get Gould and Forster."

***

Forster had lined up some Molotov cocktails by the foot of the staircase. He had taken gasoline from a spare can in the Mercedes, which they had recovered earlier and parked outside the main entrance. Everything was set for a quick getaway. Now Forster was sitting on the bottom step while Gould leaned against the ancient altar stone.

"Sorry, Gould," said Forster. "But I reckon she's dead by now."

As Gould began to protest, Forster raised his hands to placate his colleague.

"I know, time flows differently there. But even if you're right about that George bloke having spent, say, ten years there for two hundred here—that means Denny's been in the PD for, what? Half an hour, thereabouts? With no special equipment. No air support, no bio-hazard suit, no effective weapons, no back up."

Gould shook his head.

"We don't know how dangerous the PD is in small doses," he pointed out. "If it's as vast as the earth we know, she could be in no more danger than someone spending half an hour in the Sahara, or Tibet."

"Or at the South Pole in their undershorts," Forster riposted. "Be realistic—"

Both men suddenly sprang upright as the gateway darkened and a pale, spindly figure materialized. Forster raised his shotgun, but Gould warned him to hold his fire. A diminutive form fell sprawling to the stone floor with a yelp of dismay.

"Is it one of them?" demanded Forster, circling to one side of the newcomer as Gould moved closer.

Then the sphere of shimmering air became a gray blur, and Denny fell through, almost landing on top of the stranger.

"It's her!" Gould reassured Forster, then reached to help Denny to her feet. "What happened?"

"Long story, they're close behind," Denny gasped. "Help Lucy."

Gould froze, then stared down at the huddled figure on the floor by his feet. He saw now that it was a girl with long hair, wrapped in spirals of white fiber. Dark eyes looked up at his. The child was clearly terrified. There was no hint of recognition. But her face was so familiar that for a moment Gould wondered if he was dreaming.

"What?" he demanded, unsure that he had heard correctly. "Lucy?"

"It is," said Denny. "But we're going to have company in a second."

She stooped down and grabbed Lucy by the hand, then pulled her towards the staircase. Forster shouted something, taking aim at the gateway. A lithe creature appeared, materializing in the act of leaping forward, clawed hands outstretched. It was not remotely human. Gould glimpsed a nightmarish face with a circular funnel-like muzzle containing a ring of teeth.

Forster fired, catching the Interloper in the thigh. It screeched and fell, black blood spraying over Gould. He fired both barrels into the hideous face, watched its monstrous features explode into a massive gout of foul liquid and torn tissue. The Interloper writhed, limbs twitching, then grew still.

They were both reloading when the second Interloper appeared. Behind, a third was coming into view. Denny and Lucy were clambering up the stairs. The two creatures were focused on catching the fugitives. Gould shot one in the back, while Forster knocked the other down with the butt of his gun, then finished it off.

"Too many," Forster said, jerking his head at the gateway. "Retreat."

By the time the fourth Interloper had fallen into their world, Forster had lit one of his firebombs. Raising it above his head, he smashed it onto the cellar floor, directly below the portal to the Phantom Dimension. The Interloper squealed as burning gasoline sprayed over it, but still bounded forward. Gould shot it in the face. Two more bombs covered the whole area around the altar with burning liquid. The stench of burning flesh mingled with gasoline, the roar of flames not quite masking the screeches of Interlopers in their death-agony.

Gould and Forster waited at the top of the stairs until the smoke and fumes drove them out into the corridor. It was clear that nothing else would be coming through for a while.

"What the hell?" asked Jim.

"Close enough," replied Denny. "Guys, this young lady is called Lucy."

She looked at Gould, who was clearly puzzled.

"Ted," Denny said gently, "maybe now isn't the time..."

"Lucy!" Gould said, falling to his knees in front of the little girl. Tears blurred his vision as he tried to take hold of her. Lucy wriggled, began to shout in panic. Denny gently disengaged Gould's arms from the child. Lucy's eyes were wide with fear, now, and she clung to her rescuer.

"Think about it, Ted," Denny said quietly. "She hasn't seen you grow old. She still remembers the little boy who teased her."

"All fascinating and maybe heartbreaking," Forster said, not turning his gaze from the doorway. "But we have a problem when that fire burns out. Which will be soon."

"We can leave," said Jim. "The fog's lifted."

"Fog?" asked Denny.

"Tell you on the way," Jim replied.

***

"You'll be okay with Brie while I go and get you some great new clothes," said Denny. "You don't want to wear those raggedy pajamas forever, right?"

Lucy had finally stopped clinging to Denny when they had arrived in Chester. The sight of a normality, an English town bustling with shoppers, tourists, and commuters, had seemed to calm the child. Now they were in the apartment rented by Forster and Davenport, who had discreetly left 'the girls' to use it and gone with the rest of the party to find a hotel.

"I don't want you to go," Lucy pleaded, tugging at Denny's hand.

"You'll be okay with me, sweetie," said Brie, smiling down at the girl. "We can make sandwiches for lunch—or you can just watch TV. Denny will be back real soon and then we can get you dressed nicely"

Lucy looked skeptical. Denny scooped up the child and deposited her carefully on the sofa. The Phantom Dimension organism attached to her back still pulsed with alien life. The black filaments spread under the girl's skin were much more apparent in normal light. Lucy curled up, careful not to let the nodule touch the back of the sofa.

How the hell will they get that thing off her? Denny wondered, then pushed the thought aside.

"Brie's right," she said soothingly, stroking Lucy's hair. "I'll get you some cool new clothes and, in the meantime, you can get something to eat. It's a win-win situation. So, you be good, now, and do what Brie says?"

Lucy managed to smile along with Denny.

"All right," she said. "I promise."

Lucy picked up the remote and switched on the TV. The screen filled with a vista of burning buildings. At the bottom of the screen words crawled by detailing bombing raids, diplomatic overtures, stalled peace talks. Denny took the remote and searched for a cartoon channel, found something bright, noisy, and innocuous.

"I'll try not to be too long," she said, kissing the top of Lucy's head.

***

"This is a very seedy hotel," grumbled Davenport, running a finger along a picture frame. "Our expenses can't be this pathetic?"

"Nice hotels don't let you smuggle smelly, half-naked old nutters past reception, as a rule," Forster said, nodding at Lord George Blaisdell. The old nobleman was sitting on the hotel bed, enjoying a triple-decker cheeseburger and fries. An empty coffee cup stood on the bedside table.

"I know he's not had real food for a while," Davenport observed. "But still, they must have had bloody awful table manners in those old times, don't you reckon?"

"And he smells a bit," Forster added. "But I daresay they didn't bathe too often, either. Think we can persuade him to shower at some point?"

"So what's the plan, boss?" Davenport asked, raising his voice to speak to Gould, who was standing by the window gazing out at Chester's rooftops.

"Hmm?" Gould looked round. "We need to get both victims to London. The foundation's doctors might be able to figure out how to remove those—symbiotes, or whatever they are."

At that, George looked up from his meal in alarm.

"Doctors?" he exclaimed. "Barber-surgeons and apothecaries—quacks the lot of 'em! I will not let a sawbones near me. I would rather be hag-ridden by this demonic leech to my dying day, sir!"

"With all due respect, your lordship," said Davenport. "You're talking a load of bollocks. That thing might have kept you alive in the PD—in Hell, if you like—but it can't survive in our world."

"Then let it wither away of its own accord, lad!" thundered the old man. "Why tinker with it? Doctors—charlatans all."

"Now might be the time to wrong foot him," Davenport whispered to his colleague.

"You never did tell us, your lordship," said Forster, in a friendly voice, "how you managed to make such a remarkable escape. After all, it's no mean feat to get out of Hell, is it?"

George looked blank for a moment, then gave a broad, yellow-toothed smile.

"They were distracted," he said. "Moved me to a spot close to one of their magical doorways—why, I was not even a dozen yards from it! Then they left me alone, went off about other business. I managed to reach a shard of bottle glass and cut my bonds, and voila! Thus, I returned to the world of men!"

Gould turned from the window to stare at George, then exchanged glances with the other two.

"So, my lord," Gould said slowly, "you certainly enjoyed tremendous good luck."

"Fortune favors the brave," said George smugly, dipping his last curly fry in a puddle of ketchup.

"Excuse me, gents," said Gould. "I just need to step outside and make a phone call."

***

Denny went into the first store she found that sold children's clothing and headed for the section marked Girls. She made a guess at Lucy's size and bought sneakers, pants, several shirts, a jacket, and a variety of socks and underclothes. The store was busy, and Denny found herself in a long queue. In front of her a mother was trying to tell her daughter, who looked around six, that going to feed ducks in the park would be fun.

"I want to play on your iPad!" the girl kept repeating.

"We didn't have iPads in my day," the mother eventually said.

Like that's gonna work, lady, Denny thought. She smiled wryly at the way children so quickly seized on new gadgets, and how quickly adults forget that they had been just as obsessed with novelty.

Denny frowned. A thought had nearly crystallized in her mind, a nagging doubt that—she realized—had been with her for some time. Something did not quite fit. Something about the little girl and her mom's iPad. The way kids pick up new tech, new trends.

"Can I help you?" said the assistant.

Denny realized she was holding up the line and rushed forward to pay for Lucy's new things. She was just leaving the store when her phone rang. It was Gould.

"Denny," he said, in a voice that was pitched higher than usual, "how is Lucy? Is she well? Does she seem okay?"

"Yeah," Denny replied. "She seemed fine when I left her with Brie. I went out to get some clothes."

"Right," Gould said, "Jim went out to get some for George. It's about George, I'm calling, in a way. It seems like his escape was—you could call it a set-up. Contrived."

Denny felt confused, impatient, all the stress she had suffered conspiring to fog her mind. She nearly bumped into a young couple, frowned at them, stopped walking.

"Why would they do that?" she asked.

"To prepare us for Lucy's return," Gould said. "To prime our expectations. Make it seem more likely. Just as all the terror and killing was designed to confuse us, make us more susceptible to tricks."

Denny's head span with the implications.

"But that would mean they took Frankie to lure me through, simply so I would rescue Lucy—no, come on!" she protested, ignoring odd looks from passersby. "How could they possibly know—"

She paused, reflecting on the way the Interlopers understood people's deepest hopes and fears. And then the thought that had been worrying at the back of her mind sprang into the foreground, clear as daylight.

"Oh my God!" she yelled. "Lucy knew how to work the TV remote! Nobody showed her—Ted, did you have a remote, when she was still with you? Did they have those in England then?"

"No," said Gould. "Or at least, I don't think so. God, I can't remember! It was so long ago, I—"

"If it's not Lucy, she could have picked the knowledge straight out of my mind," Denny said, starting to run. "But Ted, try and remember!"

***

"Hey guys!" said Denny, trying to sound cheerful as she dumped the bags of new clothes onto the dining room table.

Lucy was still curled up on the sofa watching TV, the nodule on her back pulsing steadily. Denny could hear the low rush of water from the small bathroom.

"Hey!" Denny said. "Got you new clothes. Where's Brie?"

Lucy looked round and gave a perfect, angelic smile. She picked up the remote and muted the TV sound.

Kids are just quick learners, Denny thought. *Proves nothing. Anyway, Brie could have helped.*

"Brie's taking a shower," she said, uncurling and jumping up. "Can I try my clothes on now?"

"Of course," said Denny, resisting the urge to back away as Lucy ran over to her and grabbed her around the waist. Denny looked down at the tangled mass of chestnut hair, forced herself to pat Lucy on the shoulder.

"Okay," said Denny, "let's take the things into the bedroom."

Lucy cheerfully picked up two large bags and scampered ahead.

The bedroom was dark, its curtains drawn. Denny hesitated in the doorway.

"Lucy, you're big enough to dress yourself, now? Right?"

Lucy turned to look up at Brie, and now her face was in shadow it was impossible to read.

"Of course, I am!" she said, and closed the bedroom door.

Denny let out a sigh of relief, looked over at the sofa, and the black oblong box of the remote. Then she re-crossed the room and stopped at the bathroom door.

"Brie?" she shouted. "I'm back!"

There was no reply. Denny tried the door handle, and it opened, releasing a wave of heat and steam. The shower was of the old-fashioned type, with a curtain enclosing a bathtub rather than a glass cubicle. Denny stepped forward and pulled the gaily-colored plastic sheet aside. Brie lay in the tub fully clothed, mouth open in a silent scream. Torrents of boiling hot water were parboiling her face. The dressing on her face had been washed away, revealing the dark patch where she had been wounded the day before. A breadknife protruded from her chest.

Denny stifled a scream, staggered back into the living room. The TV screen was still radiant with the bright, colorful images of kids' cartoons. In the bedroom, Lucy stood, dressed now like a typical small girl.

Innocence in pastel shades. The thought swam into Denny mind, and as it appeared, the diminutive Interloper tilted its head to one side.

"You're very easy to read," said the entity. "But hard to scare. No real demons. Brie was much easier. I frightened her with the girl she helped to kill, so she didn't put up much of a fight."

"What do you mean?" Denny asked, partly to play for time, partly out of genuine fascination with the weird being in front of her. "No real demons?"

The thing with Lucy's face tilted its head to one side and smiled.

"Most people have a deep-rooted fear," said the Interloper. "But you are almost a blank slate. No fear to draw upon. And no frustrated dreams, either. Nothing to exploit."

Denny began to edge toward the apartment door. Lucy made a sudden leap, scarily fast like a jumping spider. It blocked Denny's escape route.

"I did make a mistake with the remote control," the Interloper said, in a flat, emotionless voice. "It was stupid. As I said, you're easy to read, so I picked the knowledge out of your head. And now look what's happened."

It took a pace forward, crouched, its face starting to elongate, while its forehead seemed to shrink.

"Now, I have to go back," said the Interloper. "And leave no loose ends. I still have plenty to report. I've seen your world first-hand, not in fragments, not distorted through your strange minds."

"Why?" asked Denny, backing away. "Why do all this? Why try to fool us?"

"To find out more about you," Lucy said, its voice growing harsher, the syllables less clearly formed. "To spy on you. It took a long time to make me. I'm very special. I can survive for weeks, months maybe. But now I won't get to see inside the foundation."

Denny still struggled to understand the lengths of scheming the Interlopers had gone to. The question 'Why' kept circling in her head, even as she glanced about for possible weapons.

"Why?" it grunted. "Because we don't like you."

It made another sudden, terrifying leap and landed squarely on Denny's chest, knocking her back against the table, which collapsed under them. Denny screamed, but the entity that was no longer anything like Lucy Gould, and put a powerful hand to her mouth.

"We don't like the way you are now," it hissed. "We don't like your machines, your cities, your science. We liked you before, when you were weak and scattered, and scared of the forests, of all the shadowed places. Then you showed us respect, you gave us nice things to leave you alone! Now you think you're gods, but you're greedy and cruel and stupid and you're spoiling everything!"

It reared up, its transformation complete, an unearthly beast brandishing vicious claws. It lowered the weirdly prehensile funnel of its muzzle towards Denny's face. It half-hissed, half-slobbered words at her that she could barely understand.

"You're killing us!"

Amid her terror, Denny felt something alien probing her mind. It was like a dark tendril, touching memories and emotions, sending a chill through her. Then the invading force stabbed deep into the roots of her identity, trying to tear apart her very essence.

"Stop!" she gasped. "Get out of my mind!"

"No," Lucy gurgled. "I need to know more before you die! You are a strange one. Mysteries!"

"No!" Denny screamed, battling Lucy with her mind and body. For all its power, the Interloper was still no heavier than a small child. Denny visualized all her anger as a glowing ball of fire, erupting from the core of her being. She hurled it at the questing black tendril. Lucy flinched at the psychic impact, startled by an impulse so immediate and primal that she could not have predicted it. Denny seized her chance, broke the creature's grip, bringing up both knees to hurl it across the room. Lucy crashed into the TV screen. But even as Denny was scrambling upright, the Interloper had recovered, and knocked her down again.

"Simpler to kill you," it said.

The muzzle-mouth opened revealing a circle of long, thin teeth that turned outward. Denny struggled frantically but this time the grip of the Interloper's wiry arms and legs had immobilized her. She closed her eyes and twisted her head to the side, feeling the creature's hot breath on her face. But the pain that came next was not the kind she had expected. A jolt shot through her, and she arched her back in a spasm. The grip of the Interloper relaxed, and Denny heard a bestial screech followed by a sickening blow.

When she opened her eyes, Gould and Forster was standing over her. Gould was holding a taser, while the other man was putting down a shotgun with a bloodied butt. The creature had collapsed, and Denny easily heaved the Interloper off her and scrambled away from it.

"I didn't think it would be wise to blow her head off," remarked Forster, almost casually. "Besides, taking them alive might get me a bonus."

Gould bent over the tiny figure. The body was face down. He turned it over cautiously with his foot, taser at the ready, but the Interloper did not move. The eyes, now tiny black beads in deep, pale sockets, gazed blankly upward. A yellowish froth had formed around the mouth. Gould looked up at Denny.

"I think she's dead,"

"You mean *it's* dead," corrected Forster.

"Yeah," said Gould, looking down at the body in its incongruous child's outfit. "Yeah, that's what I meant."

"I'll get something from the van to wrap it in," Forster said. "Best keep clear of it, just in case."

After he left, Gould sat down and buried his face in his hands.

"I'm sorry," said Denny. "It must have been so hard to admit that it wasn't her."

Gould looked up, tears streaming down his face.

"I so wanted to believe," he said. "Right up to the moment we came through that door. I wanted to see her there. An innocent child."

He covered his face again, giving a great, heaving sob.

"We'll find her," Denny said firmly, sitting by him and putting an arm around his shoulders. "We'll find them both."

THE ROMOLA FOUNDATION

"I hate clearing up, it's so boring," said Davenport, climbing out of the van and surveying the house with distaste. "You sure the police are finished?"

"Yeah," replied Forster. "Property is now back in the hands of our lovely foundation."

"Will bricking up that doorway do the job?" asked Davenport, gesturing at a group of builders standing by a truck.

"That's not the plan," the older man corrected. "This time they're going to fill the cellar with concrete. Right up to the ceiling."

This gave Davenport pause for thought.

"So the little buggers won't be able to get out, into our world, ever again?"

Forster gave a weak smile, gestured at the great house. They started to walk up the steps to the palatial front door.

"Look, son, this is just one site. The foundation's identified dozens around the country, and dozens more overseas. We can't shut them out completely. But it sends a message."

Davenport muttered a few colorful versions of what that message might be. Inside they found that the police had removed all the investigators' belongings. The Interloper remains had been dealt with before the police had been called in. The two men went over the house room by room, looking for anything significant, but drew a blank.

"So," said Davenport, looking around him. "Is that it? Are we done?"

"Not quite," Forster said, leading him back to the cellar entrance. "Just a picture to take. I almost forgot, but you know how Benson likes everything strange documented."

In the corridor near the doorway, Forster pointed up at the wall. The message to Brie that had been scratched into the plaster was still legible.

"Oh, that," Davenport said, dismissively. "I got a shot of that the first time. And the other one."

Forster nodded absently, then frowned.

"What other one?"

This time it was the younger man's turn to lead his superior. Just outside the kitchen, there was a similar array of deep scars in the plasterwork, just above head height. The light was poor, and even using a flashlight Forster struggled to make out the words.

"I reckon it's a threat, kind of," said Davenport.

"Or just an observation," Forster mused, raising his camera to take the image. "Right, let's pack up and get out of this dump."

On the way back to headquarters, the two chatted about trivial matters, as always, rather than the grimmer aspects of their unusual work. But that night, when he was back at home with his family, Forster found it hard to focus on his kid's chatter about school or his wife's complaints about her boss. His thoughts kept returning to the enigmatic message scored deep into the fabric of Malpas Abbey.

THERE ARE WORSE THINGS THAN US

***

"The film from the obsolete camera you recovered has been processed," said Benson.

"So I gathered," replied Gould.

Benson raised a hand, and the lights dimmed. A low-grade, black and white film flickered on the screen. A group of men in old-fashioned British army uniforms were shown in front of a bricked-up doorway.

"Medical orderlies, I take it?" asked Benson.

"Yes," agreed Gould. "Members of the Royal Army Medical Corps.

The house was earmarked as an infirmary for wounded officers immediately after World War One."

"Hmm," said Benson. "Hence the desire to put the cellar to use."

"For storage space, probably," said Gould. "An unwise decision."

A couple of them raised hammers, knocked a way through. The film then cut to a scene in the cellar of Malpas Abbey, with two of the orderlies horsing around by the altar. A close-up followed, showing one man pulling a funny face next to the carvings on the pale stone.

"All good clean fun," observed Benson. "But I'm assuming the entire establishment, at this point, was full of men who had suffered considerable trauma on the Western Front?"

"Yes," said Gould. "Each with his personal demons."

The film suddenly became jerky as the man who had been fooling around stood up and looked at something out of camera shot. The point of view veered wildly, then came to rest on what looked like a ball of mist, hovering in the air. A dark shape formed inside the sphere, then leaped forward. The picture span, then the camera must have struck the floor and ended up on its side. A struggle was under way, but those involved were out of focus. Then a figure came into view, for a brief moment.

"They enhanced this image," said Benson. "Quite graphic."

The Interloper was a conventional image of Death, a skeletal figure with a skull-like visage. Much of the detail was lost in a blur of movement, but it was clear that one of the creature's claws was in the act of scooping the innards out of a still-living man. The soldier's face was frozen in a scream of agony.

"The terrifying death they had escaped in the trenches of Flanders came to claim them in England," Benson commented. "Almost poetic. But of no real practical value for our research."

"No," agreed Gould, his mouth suddenly dry. "I suppose not. Though..."

Gould hesitated, glanced at the man in the dark suit.

"You have one of your theories, perhaps?" asked Benson quietly.

"We assume they deliberately draw on our emotions and memories," said Gould carefully. "But what if it's a two-way process? What if our obsessions, nightmares, fantasies, shape their appearance and behavior regardless of what they might want?"

Benson looked at Gould for a moment, gave a slight nod.

"And some people would be more influential than others. Your friend Ms. Purcell, for instance, seems to have no personal demons to evoke. But you may be barking up the wrong tree, Gould. Not for the first time."

"It's just a hypothesis," murmured Gould.

"Quite—and now for something completely different," Benson said, raising his hand again so that his long fingers were illuminated by the projector beam.

The black and white image was replaced by modern digital video. Gould saw himself, Denny, Matt, all in a state of confusion as an Interloper bounded down the steps into Blaisdell's temple. There was confused shouting. The field up vision spun, swung upwards as Frankie struggled with the creature that grabbed her from behind, then the second Interloper blocked the view as it leaped at her. There was a whirl of chaotic motion, a screeching sound, then blackness and silence.

"The transition is, as always, impossible to record with any clarity," murmured Benson, with a trace of frustration. "Perhaps with specialized equipment."

"Quite," agreed Gould.

Now the screen showed a bleak, outlandish scene, one Gould recognized from Denny's description. The camera fell to the ground, and pairs of feet—some human, some not—appeared briefly. There was a howling that suggested a strong wind, plus scuffling and the faint sound of Frankie's voice. Her cries dwindled quickly, then were gone. A couple of seconds ticked by on the digital readout in the corner of the screen. Then the camera was lifted and Denny's face, huge and distorted by proximity, appeared for a moment.

"The young woman showed great courage and initiative at this juncture," said Benson. "I agree that she may be an asset. Intriguing that she might be able to block the enemy's psychic powers. Training could help with that. And of course, it is better to have her inside the organization, rather than out in the world telling her story. She is impulsive, though. You'll have to watch that."

The viewpoint swung around as Denny panned around the unearthly vista, then settled on a vague object on the horizon. The camera zoomed in, but the peculiar light and the sheer distance meant the image remained blurred.

"Again," Benson said, "our people managed to remove much of the noise from one frame and get a clear picture."

The still image came up on the screen. Gould gave an involuntary gasp of horror.

"Despite its size, this object is, our experts think, a living thing rather than a machine. But whatever it is, it is most certainly heading for the gateway," Benson remarked. "And moving quite fast, considering its size. We must be thankful that it will take a good while to get there. Years, one hopes."

"But," Gould began. "There are so many other gateways!"

"Indeed," Benson said. "We must, as usual, hope for the best while we prepare for the worst. These—colossal entities could be emerging all over the world in the very near future. The human race would find it difficult to deal with them given our present state of chronic disorganization."

***

After parting company with Benson, Gould went to the Knightsbridge Hilton, where Denny had been booked at the foundation's expense. They had used a false name, as the killings of three people and the disappearance of a fourth had embroiled them in a media feeding frenzy. The loss of almost all of its personnel had, ironically, made 'America's Weirdest Hauntings' a ratings success again.

"What about the cops?" asked Denny, as they sat down for coffee in a quiet corner of the bar. "They thought I was crazy when I started talking about monsters. Eventually I just clammed up and they got some doctor to say I was suffering from PTSD."

"Which is why I didn't talk about monsters," said Gould gently. "Jim and I worked out a version of events that makes it seem—without saying it in so many words—that Frankie is a deranged serial killer, currently on the run."

"That's ludicrous!" Denny protested. "How can they be dumb enough to buy that?"

"Because their dumb theory doesn't involve monsters," Gould riposted. "Do you want to try telling them the truth again? Or maybe go to our wonderful British newspaper with your story?"

Denny shrugged.

"I might have to sell my story. No show, no job."

Gould looked around the bar, then leaned closer.

"The Romola Foundation would like to offer you a job," he said. "As part of my team of investigators."

Denny sat open-mouthed, coffee half-raised to her lips. She put the cup down carefully, then asked, "Does that mean I might get to go after Frankie again?"

Gould nodded.

"And you're still hoping to find Lucy," she went on. "Right?"

Gould looked out of the window at the skyline of London. It was a pleasant autumn day, sunshine glinting on the capital's tower blocks.

"I have to hope," he said. "We both do. And you've proven yourself. More than proved. If there's such a thing as a natural at this game, you're it."

Denny paused for a moment, then smiled up at Gould.

"Okay, you got a deal," she said, holding out her hand. "Say, did you get anything useful from Frankie's camera? I saw some crazy shit over there."

"No—no, we didn't," said Gould, shaking her hand firmly. "I'm afraid the memory was wholly corrupted. The physics team thinks it was a side-effect of the transition—something to do with quantum entanglement. Or so they tell me."

"Oh, crap," moaned Denny. "Better luck next time, I guess."

***

In a white, windowless room, Lord George Blaisdell lay strapped to a metal couch. The unusually shaped frame supported his weight without crushing the organism fastened between his shoulder blades.

"He is still conscious, Wickes?" asked Benson, observing Blaisdell through a narrow slit in a padded door.

"Yes, sir," said Doctor Wickes. "Though he drifts in an out of delirium. His grasp on reality is somewhat fragile."

"Not surprising," Benson said. "And the PD entity? Is it simply a parasite?"

Wickes shook her head.

"Definitely not, sir. As far as we can tell, it is symbiotic. We assume it was affixed to his body specifically to allow him to survive for a prolonged period in the PD. Much as we might keep an animal specimen alive in an artificial environment."

Benson peered through the slit for a few seconds, then turned to face his chief biologist.

"In other words, that strange lump of tissue feeds him?"

"Quite right, sir," said Wickes, with a slightly nervous smile. "It has altered his biophysical structure so that it can somehow process compounds from the PD into nutrients."

"Fascinating," said Benson, firmly. "But can it be transferred to one of our operatives?"

Wickes looked more nervous, her eyes wide.

"Sir, it is part of his body now. We think that removing the symbiote would cause massive metabolic shock, possibly fatal."

Benson looked levelly at Wickes until the latter lowered her eyes.

"Get on with it. And do not use anesthetic. You don't know what effect such chemicals might have on that thing."

"But—" Wickes began. "If we kill him?"

"He's been legally dead for a long time," Benson replied. "Think of it as a kind of post-mortem."

Wickes signaled to a pair of orderlies standing nearby. Then she went to a long table that stood against the wall. Surgical instruments and a box of latex gloves were laid out ready.

When they opened the door, Blaisdell began to shout and writhe in his bonds.

"Turn him over, quickly," ordered Wickes.

The orderlies rotated the metal frame until the captive's back was facing upwards. Wickes took a deep breath and raised a scalpel. She began to cut away the flesh around the unearthly organism. The brown hemisphere pulsed and quivered as black fluid spurted from severed vessels. Blaisdell screamed.

"I thought I had escaped from Hell, but I was wrong!"

***

"Classic case of overkill, if you ask me," said the guard, checking Forster's pass. "Waste of my time. But hey, I'm getting paid."

Forster looked the man up and down, then stepped past him to the cell door. He opened the viewing slit and stood peering inside for half a minute. Then he closed the aperture and stood in silence for a few moments.

"Overkill," said Forster eventually. "Interesting term. Very applicable in this particular case."

The guard looked uncertain as Forster looked him over.

"If anything," Forster said, "I think it's a case of underkill to have just one bloke on guard outside this particular door. You know the procedure, right?"

"Of course, chief," the guard replied, sounding slightly aggrieved. "If our guest starts getting lively, I report it at once."

"You hit the panic button," corrected Forster. "Grade One alert. Your first priority is to get help down here. Don't try to do anything on your own."

The guard nodded, and Forster started to walk away towards the security checkpoint at the end of the corridor.

"Er, chief," said the guard.

Forster stopped and turned, raised an eyebrow at the young man.

"Yes? Something not clear?"

The guard shuffled his feet, reddened slightly.

"It's just," he said. "Well, it just seems a bit weird. I mean, why's that thing dressed like a little girl?"

* * *

If you enjoyed the book, please leave a review. Your reviews inspire us to continue writing about the world of spooky and untold horrors!

Check out these best-selling books from our talented authors

Ron Ripley (Ghost Stories)
- Berkley Street Series Books 1 – 9
  www.scarestreet.com/berkleyfullseries
- Moving in Series Box Set Books 1 – 6
  www.scarestreet.com/movinginboxfull

A. I. Nasser (Supernatural Suspense)
- Slaughter Series Books 1 – 3 Bonus Edition
  www.scarestreet.com/slaughterseries

David Longhorn (Sci-Fi Horror)
- Nightmare Series: Books 1 – 3
  www.scarestreet.com/nightmarebox
- Nightmare Series: Books 4 – 6
  www.scarestreet.com/nightmare4-6

Sara Clancy (Supernatural Suspense)
- Banshee Series Books 1 – 6
  www.scarestreet.com/banshee1-6

For a complete list of our new releases and best-selling horror books, visit www.scarestreet.com/books

See you in the shadows,
Team Scare Street